A SHIELD MAIDEN'S EARL

Of Scots and Vikings, Book 1

By

Sky Purington

ARE YOU SIGNED UP FOR DRAGONBLADE'S BLOG?

You'll get the latest news and information on exclusive giveaways, exclusive excerpts, coming releases, sales, free books, cover reveals and more.

Check out our complete list of authors, too!

No spam, no junk. That's a promise!

Sign Up Here

www.dragonbladepublishing.com

Dearest Reader;

Thank you for your support of a small press. At Dragonblade Publishing, we strive to bring you the highest quality Historical Romance from some of the best authors in the business. Without your support, there is no 'us', so we sincerely hope you adore these stories and find some new favorite authors along the way.

Happy Reading!

CEO, Dragonblade Publishing

Additional Dragonblade books by Author Sky Purington

Of Scots and Vikings Series
A Shield Maiden's Earl (Book 1)

Second Time Brides Series
Never Second Guess a Lord (Book 1)
The Secondhand Earl (Book 2)
Second Thoughts about the Heir (Book 3)
Harrowing Hall (Novella)

Highlander's Pact Series
Scoundrel's Vengeance (Book 1)
Scoundrel's Fortune (Book 2)
Scoundrel's Redemption (Book 3)

The Lyon's Den Series
To Tame the Lyon

Pirates of Britannia Series
The Seafaring Rogue
The Sea Hellion

When a fierce shield-maiden touched by the Valkyries is forced to marry a powerful Norwegian earl, fiery passion ignites, and destiny unfolds.

Freya—Born of seers and Vikings of old, I never could have imagined my father someday ordering me to hand over my shield and blade to the man he made me wed. Nor could I have fathomed that man would be Earl Soren Dahl. A warrior chieftain known for his battle prowess and incredible feats, who has long wanted me. When he arrives on my shores to claim me, I expect to despise him, yet he sets my blood afire. More telling, my mystical talisman claims we are fated.

Soren—From the moment I laid eyes on Freya Helvig, as a child, I knew she would someday be mine. Though it took years of making a name for myself and building my tribe into one of the most formidable strongholds in the Kingdom of Norway, I finally claimed her. Or at least I tried. My beautiful, feisty bride-to-be is a force to be reckoned with. A force I welcome, ready to go to battle and conquer her heart, no matter what it takes.

Brought together by the Norns, Freya and Soren navigate the ever-changing landscape of thirteenth-century Scandinavia, amid love and destiny. Brought together and torn apart by the whims of magic and mortal men, by King Hákon and the Battle of Largs, ushering in the beginning of the end of Norse rule over Scotland. Will Freya and Soren be lost to each other in the end? Or will they survive all that's determined to separate them?

Dedication

This series is dedicated to my cousin and dear friend, Michelle.

Here's to Siberian huskies, brilliant ideas, and tales of old!

PROLOGUE

Freya

11 February 1243
Storskog, Kingdom of Norway
Norwegian-Russian border

"DO YOU SEE it?" Tucking a curl behind my ear, I squinted through the driving snow as my sisters, Astrid and Tove, and I trudged through the deepening drifts toward home. I spotted something small and dark moving up ahead and was surprised when I recognized what it was. "Just ahead in the woodland," I gasped. "'Tis a gray wolf pup."

Although I should have been frightened, since a wolf pup was bound to have a mother nearby, I felt no such fear. Instead, as the frigid wind gusted and towering oak and spruce trees creaked and groaned overhead, I was drawn to it, sensing it was here to deliver a message.

"We should not approach it," cautioned Astrid, the youngest of us. Her unruly mass of honey blond locks blew every which way, and her pale blue eyes rounded with worry. "Father would not like it."

"Yet Father is not here," reminded my older sister, Tove, always the most daring.

"No, he's not," I agreed, swearing I caught a glint of metal near the pup. Edging closer, we remained watchful of our surroundings lest a larger wolf appear. "I think it has something in its mouth."

"*Ja.*" Astrid's eyes grew wider still. "'Tis a *blade.*"

As if responding to her words, the wolf dropped the dagger and trotted off. More curious than ever, we pulled our furs tightly around us to ward off the wind's chill and approached the area.

"There's nothing there," Astrid exclaimed once we reached the location.

"Yet there is," Tove said softly, crouching where an impression of a blade dented the snow. She ignored her thick, blue-black hair whipping in the wind and reached down with her gloved hand, her usual fearless self. Furrowing her brow in concentration, she felt around in the snow until she found what she was looking for and then lifted out the most magnificent dagger we had ever seen.

"'Tis of the gods," she whispered, awestruck at the Nordic designs aglow along its well-forged steel. Gifted in the way of ancient seers, her eyes hazed with a mystical darkness, and her voice took on the octave of our shield-maiden ancestors. "'Tis of the Valkyries and our destinies. Of our great purpose, warrior spirits, and fates we must follow to distant shores and o marriages that will divide us, yet things we *must* see through."

"But we are too young to marry," Astrid whispered, as if she didn't want to say it too loudly and offend the gods.

"Right now," I murmured, feeling my inner seer stir. "But someday we will be old enough and 'twill be time."

"And how will we know when that is?" Astrid cocked her head. "Is it not Father's role to see us married?"

"'Tis and 'twill be," Tove said, feeling the same stirring as I when the wind whipped around us. As if the gods spoke to her, she lowered the blade beneath the snow again. When she lifted her hand, the blade had morphed into three small stones attached to leather strings. "Yet these talismans will be at the root of it."

After urging us to duck behind a boulder out of the wind, she hung a dark blue stone around my neck, a dark green stone around Astrid's, and a dark purplish black stone around her own neck.

As the years passed, Tove's predictions proved accurate, and we embarked on our journeys through life. Ones that would indeed take us to distant shores and mark the beginning of significant change coming for both Vikings and Scots alike.

CHAPTER ONE

Freya

13 May 1263
Moskenesøya Isle, Norway

"I CAN DO this," I told myself under my breath. "I have no choice."

Now was not the time for weakness but strength, as I approached Tove's cottage. I knew I should only ever be strong when dealing with my eldest sister, or, for that matter, our father. Yet still, when I entered my sister's cottage to spend these last few hours together before the Norns ripped us apart, it wasn't easy. It was heart-wrenching.

Even so, such emotions had no room in these precious few moments. Any more than they had when we spent our last few hours with our sister, Astrid, before she'd departed for Scotland the previous year.

Practicing the foreign tongue of English, because, like my sisters, I knew it would become more common where we traveled, I forced a smile, somehow managing to keep my tears at bay. "Hello, Tove."

My sister had braided her thick, black hair. Her pale, sea-green eyes were impossible to read. Nodding hello curtly from where she sat in front of a crackling fire at the center of her cottage, she gestured that I shut the door behind me, then did the last thing I expected. She left her chair and quickly closed the distance to embrace me tightly.

Relieved that I could let my guard down and return her affection, I embraced her just as tightly, trembling at the impact of these final, bittersweet moments. Fleeting moments, before we went our separate ways. We might never see each other again, something Tove seemed to understand, because I felt a tremor go through her too. Then, just as swiftly as she'd embraced me, she pulled away and returned to being distant, as if the tender exchange hadn't happened.

With good reason, too.

She'd sensed our father coming.

Moments later, he pounded on the door and entered before Tove had a chance to respond. A once-tall, formidable man and ruthless warrior, Earl Bjǫrn Helvig, 'The Ferocious,' had at one time been renowned for his battle prowess, yet was now a husk of the man he'd been. Stooped, terribly scarred, and in more pain than he would admit, he wore an angry scowl where once, at least for his daughters, there had been a warm smile. With the assistance of his second-in-command, Knud, he lowered into one of the chairs around the fire with a muttered grunt and accepted a mug of ale from Tove.

Knud Thorngard was a towering monster of a man with broad shoulders, a lightning bolt scar at his temple, and a more-than-imposing bearing. He had risen to the rank of our father's trusted second-in-command when he'd saved him from the polar bear that nearly took his life. Though many women found Knud handsome with his thick, dark brown hair and braided beard, including, I suspected, Tove, I found him unnerving. He hovered on a violent, beastly edge from which, if he ever crossed over, he might never return.

To that end, I had long known Knud was a great deal of the reason why Bjǫrn had not married off Tove yet. Outside of himself, she was the only one who seemed able to tame him. As for our father, although he never took offense at the bear that attacked him, having long fashioned his tribe of berserker warriors after the polar bear and proudly wearing its white pelt, his disposition changed drastically afterward.

He went from loving and doting to this, the man who narrowed his near-obsidian eyes at me and looked me over as if I were prized cattle about to be auctioned off.

But then, in a way, I very much was.

"Are you ready for him, girl?" he rasped, his shredded vocal cords making impossible the booming, commanding voice that was once his. He noted my impressive shield of blues and the well-sharpened blade I kept sheathed at my side. "You seem prepared, yet still I will have you recite your duties on behalf of your people when you greet Soren on the morrow."

Feeling my blue talisman stone warm against my skin beneath my tunic, I dutifully listed off everything my father wanted to hear. Everything I knew the gods wanted me to adhere to, as my time to marry and face my destiny would soon be upon me.

Face the man destined to be with me for the rest of my days.

"When Earl Soren Dahl, 'The Brazen,' arrives on the morrow, I shall greet him as the wife who will soon belong to him," I recited, loathing every word, yet what choice did I have? Not only was my father ordering it, but my talisman agreed.

According to the Norns, this was my fate.

The only path I could walk.

"Soren will spend time among our people," I went on, "and receive your blessing, Father, before we travel to his stronghold and marry among his tribe."

Bjǫrn was too feeble to make the journey to the Dahl stronghold, and it was only proper that I marry there, so though untraditional, we had to do things this way.

"And then," Father prompted when I hoped to leave it at that because I especially loathed the next part.

"And then," I forced past my lips, "I will dutifully bear him many children, sealing the unification of our earldoms."

"*Ja*," Father grunted, perking a bushy gray eyebrow, "but first?"

I sensed, rather than saw, my sister tense. This response was the most important of all, and the most unnatural, given I was every bit a shield-maiden.

Yet I would not say it without a bite to my voice.

"Upon greeting him, I shall hand my shield and blade over to Soren to show I will honor our upcoming vows," I swore through clenched teeth, dreading the moment. It would feel so wrong. Not like me in the least. "Despite my being an esteemed warrior who could greatly improve his ranks, and mayhap he should be told such, I will—"

"*Not* say such," my father bit out, his scarred face growing redder at my daring to say anything that countered his wishes. "You will say what I want said without any of your foolishness, girl, do you hear me?" His eyes narrowed to obsidian slits. "You are privileged enough to wed the fiercely renowned Soren Dahl, Ruler of the Ulfhednar, whose last wife bore him no sons. But you will, and strong sons at that. Sons born of our bloodline who will long watch over the Kingdom of Norway and expand well onto the distant shores of other lands. *Rule* distant lands."

While that sounded admirable enough, there was once a time Father would have wanted that to happen with me fighting alongside his warriors. Fighting as he had trained me to fight in my youth, with the spirit of a shield-maiden and the ferociousness of the bear. With the might of a thousand Helvig's because our tribe was fierce, indeed.

Yet now, I was to lay down my shield to bear sons.

Lay down who I was, at my core, for my father.

Where once I might have taken great pride in that, however difficult to grasp, because I loved my father dearly, that time had passed with Bjørn's changed disposition. Even so, as my gaze flickered from his beast, Knud, with his muscular arms crossed over his broad chest, eyeing me darkly, to the veins bulging in Father's now beet-red face, I had no choice but to swallow my pride and heartache and do as he asked.

Forcing myself to nod in acquiescence, however tightly, I

continue saying all the words my father longed—*demanded*—to hear. Then, after being dismissed so that Bjǫrn might speak alone with Knud and Tove, I made my way back to my cottage beneath a waxing moon, enjoying the woodsy hint of spring on the tepid, salt-ridden winds.

That is, until I sensed something watching me and slowed, watchful of the surrounding forest. Although close to the sea, there was enough woodland to support wildlife, so somehow I wasn't surprised when I caught the glittering eyes of my gray wolf watching me from the darkness.

Even though it made no sense, the wolf pup we'd seen in the snow had somehow followed me from the northernmost reaches of the mainland to an isle off the coast. Appearing grown, he never approached, nor brought another mystical Viking blade, but only ever watched me from afar. Comforted me. Gave me strength as if he knew I would need it.

And now here came Soren, known in some circles as the Earl of Wolves. How else could it be, given his tribe was now infamously named for *Ulfhednar*, a mystical group of warriors said to wear the skin of wolves and fight just as ferociously?

As mine and the wolf's gazes held, I couldn't help but remember Soren when we were younger. I had pointed out my wolf to him during one of his father's visits to our tribe. Little could I have ever imagined I would someday have to marry that scrawny, ebony-haired boy, once so determined to befriend and protect me despite being shorter and terrible at wielding a blade.

It seemed like a lifetime since I'd last seen him. I could hardly envision him becoming as fierce a warrior as they claimed upon inheriting his father's earldom, but he had. More than that, he'd requested my hand in marriage after the untimely death of his wife.

It was a sound move to be sure, uniting the wolf with the bear, yet still.

I would no longer be the berserker shield-maiden bear Father had raised me to be, but something else. Someone different and foreign who I despised with every fiber of my being. With every nuance of my soul. I would be something in servitude to a wolf, when ironically, a wolf had only ever given me strength.

The wolf coming for me now was far different from the one who kept watch over me, and I kept that in mind the next morning when the horns blared, announcing approaching longships. Although tempted to dress in the more comfortable trousers I often wore when battling, I knew better. I wore what my father had requested: a linen dress with the plush white fur cloak of a polar bear draped over my shoulders.

Standing tall with my chin held high, I joined my kin at the shore, relishing the feel of the cold wind, wishing it were caressing my cheeks as I sailed my own boat in the opposite direction.

"You did *not* do your hair nor your face paint as Father wished," Tove seethed under her breath when she fell in beside me. "He will not be pleased."

"No, but this is how it needs to be," I replied softly, with just as much venom. It would infuriate Father, but this was my life, too, and I was about to hand over my inner warrior to another. About to give up everything I was, my very being, for another, and I would see it done properly.

I would have Soren see me as I was before I became his.

Fortunately, my father, in his feeble state, had little opportunity to scold me or even order me to change my hair and face upon Soren's arrival. The ships were already docking, and it was too late.

Soren would see all of me. Who I *should* be. Not what he intended to turn me into. So, I made my way down to the dock on the craggy, roughly strewn shoreline and waited proudly as the lead ship approached with the last thing I expected to see.

A man at the helm wearing a black fur cloak over his shoulders and with a real and sizeable black wolf by his side.

A ripple of awe resounded on the shore where many had come to witness such an esteemed arrival. The man leapt off the ship with his wolf following behind, the two at ease in a way predator and prey should not be. Yet as his long strides brought him closer, it became clear they were one in a way that spoke to his confidence and comradeship with the animal.

The wolf drew my attention so completely with its sheer size, it took a moment to look at the man again until he was right there, as tall, broad, and imposing as my father's beast, Knud. Although he had come to a halt in front of Bjørn, who stood just ahead of me, and introduced himself as Soren Dahl, it was hard to focus on their brief conversation when all I could think of was how much he had changed.

Gone was the awkward, gangly lad of our youth. Instead, there was a strong and impressive man. It was easy to see that yes, now he was a formidable warrior. He wore a black leather tunic and trousers, along with heavy black boots. His thick hair was still a rich ebony obsidian, but his face had grown fine indeed, with chiseled features and a strong, bearded chin.

My father greeted him in turn, commenting on how much he had changed, clearly pleased by him but not so much by me. So said the frustration in his gaze when he stepped aside to allow me to do as he had bidden. He was right to be frustrated with me, too. As Tove had noticed, instead of leaving my hair down, I had intricately braided it as if going to battle, and my face paint was for war rather than to emphasize my features to please a man.

While I wasn't happy about this, my talisman was warm against my chest, telling me this was my destined path, and that Soren was part of my Wyrd. So, forcing myself to put one foot in front of the other, I made my way to him and wasted no time with the pleasant formalities I'd ensured my father I would execute, but the opposite. Although not entirely uncivil because Soren had done me no harm thus far, I stopped in front of him, nodded once in greeting, and held out my shield and blade to him, hilt first.

"Although I will *always* be a warrior, I give these to you as a show of goodwill," I managed. "Might there only ever be peace betwixt us."

"Only ever peace, then?" The corner of his mouth curled up, and his stormy, bluish-gray eyes twinkled with amusement in a way I recognized from when we were young. "Would that not grow boring after a time, Freya Helvig?"

Caught off guard by the heat curling through me at the look of promise in his gaze as he took me in with blatant admiration, I was unsure how to reply. I had expected him to be a more callous, ruthless sort, given his notorious conquests. More serious and commanding, seeing how men so swiftly followed him into battle. And I certainly had not expected to be so attracted to him when that was the last thing I wanted to feel.

Yet as his gaze lingered on my face and he awaited a response, there could be no doubt something fluctuated between us. Something that admittedly made marrying him seem less awful. That is, until I remembered I was handing him things that meant a great deal to me. Keeping that in mind, I hardened my expression and again motioned for him to accept my shield and blade.

"Whilst I appreciate your show of goodwill," he went on when he realized I wouldn't be answering, "I think you would find keeping your weapons more helpful, given you are a shield-maiden, are you not?"

Startled because I had by no means expected his reply, I arched my eyebrows and found my tongue. "Do you not want my gifts, then?"

"Surely he does," my father exclaimed, frowning at Soren. "You are here for a wife, not a warrior, *ja*? My daughter is a fine woman who will give you *many* strong sons."

"I don't doubt that." Soren continued looking at me with unmistakable appreciation. "Yet I see no reason why she cannot keep her prized shield and blade while doing so." His gaze lingered on my face for another moment before he looked at my father with a furrowed brow. "Might their mother not set a better example for our strong sons if she were a warrior?"

When my father was rendered momentarily speechless, I couldn't help but wonder if he remembered feeling the same way at one time. If he recalled, he had once wanted the same kind of wife and had raised his daughters to be just like her. Strong and fearless. Warriors who could not only defend themselves but also others. Would this moment help him remember who he once was? What he once wanted?

It turned out it did, but not in the way I expected.

CHAPTER TWO

Soren

SINCE RECEIVING WORD from Bjǫrn Helvig that he'd accepted my marriage proposal to his daughter, Freya, I had been eager, if not desperate, to see her again, longing to gaze upon the woman who had haunted my dreams for years.

And I could safely say I was not disappointed when I did.

Freya was as beautiful as ever, wearing her warrior paint, standing proudly with a fearless gleam in her thickly lashed, pale amber eyes. While of average height, she'd always had a way of seeming taller. Her thick, braided hair was still a warm crimson hue, reminiscent of a vivid sunset, and her delicate, flawless features were aglow, speaking to time spent in the late winter sun on the seas.

Although it had been many years since we'd last met as children, I was as drawn to her now as I had been when younger. She stood behind her father on the dock when, at one time, Bjǫrn would have insisted she and her sister stand beside him.

Yet, as I went through the formalities of greeting her father and noting how frail and wary Bjǫrn had become, undoubtedly due to his substantial wounds, it occurred to me there was more to his actions than one might realize. Something confirmed when the older man bit out his thoughts on my insistence that Freya keep her prized shield and blade when she tried to offer them to me.

"I agreed to this marriage for the strong sons my daughter will bear you and my Helvig lineage, Soren," Bjǫrn made clear, speaking more callously about his daughter than he would have in the past. "Not that I might hand over one of my most precious possessions so that you could use her on the battlefield to advance your own causes."

"Yet are my causes not the same as yours?" I reminded, having had no intention of sending Freya off to battle unless she wanted to go. "Do we not explore and fight on behalf of our king, Hákon Hákonarson? He who has brought this country to greatness and formed friendships with not just the Pope but the Holy Roman Emperor? A king who was even offered the imperial crown by the Pope, the High Kingship of Ireland by a delegation of Irish kings, and the command of the French crusader fleet by the French king?"

Clearly not pleased but still able-minded enough to counter well, Bjǫrn's face grew redder as he eyed me.

"*Ja*, our causes are the same," Bjǫrn conceded, giving Freya a sharp look when she thought to sheath her blade and resecure her shield. "Yet you defeat your own argument, do you not, Soren? Our good king has taken our beloved country far and, in turn, made diplomacy more favored and the battles of old less necessary. Our prized Norwegian women of fine bloodlines don't need to fight our wars anymore but serve to continue our lineage so that Norway might only ever flourish, making them treasured, indeed." He gestured at Freya. "And few are more treasured than a daughter of the fabled Helvigs and the fierce bears that watch over us."

While I agreed it was unlikely Freya would need to battle, I knew from the fierce look in her eyes it would be a poor start to our marriage if I didn't continue disputing this on her behalf. I also knew in that uncanny way I could sometimes, when it came to people's behaviors, that Bjǫrn spoke out of fear more than anything.

Fear of losing his daughter or seeing her suffer the pain he had suffered, of that I wasn't as certain. Still, most could not see such as did I in the concerned, troubled glances Bjørn shot in Freya's direction when he thought no one looked. I saw in them a man who had suffered in unimaginable ways and would be stubborn in his need not to see his daughters suffer the same. A man who once would have encouraged them to battle, mayhap even die in battle if meant embracing their shield-maiden spirits and being ushered proudly into the great halls of Valhalla.

I also saw a man who would not honor this arrangement unless he got his way. My best path forward would be to buy time and think through how best to please both Freya and her father.

"'Tis true, Freya is more treasured than most," I agreed, beginning with what meant most to her. "To that end, Bjørn Helvig, I request that for now, you allow Freya to keep her prized weapons, so that we might share an ale by a warm fire and discuss how things should proceed."

Bjørn's dark gaze remained narrowed on me before he took in all with which I had traveled: my sizeable wolf, who sat at attention by my side, his thick black pelt rippling in the wind, my four well-built, impressive ships and my equally remarkable warriors tying off and lowering the sails. I would bring a lot to this marriage. Would I be worth turning away over something so trivial?

"As you wish," Bjørn finally grunted, gesturing that Freya and I join him for the walk back to his stronghold tucked in a fog-steeped fjord and that Knud and Tove oversee my men settling in. "We will enjoy an ale in my lodge, then make our way to the celebrations if our discussions go well."

"Should I not remain by your side, my liege?" Knud asked Bjørn, seeming unsettled he had been ordered to do otherwise.

"No," Bjørn snapped, narrowing his eyes at his man as if he should have known better than to ask. "See after Earl Soren's men, then await me in the great lodge." His gaze softened on Tove despite the same warning in his voice. "Both of you."

With that, he set off with a limp to his gait, and Freya and I fell in alongside him. Doing my best not to focus on her earthy, sweet scent or the fluid movements of her lithe body, I took in the bustling seaside village. As any thriving community would, this spoke to good leadership despite Bjǫrn's scowl and curt mannerisms. Actions that I suspected were not unique to this situation.

To be expected, everyone's attention turned our way, not only due to who I was, but because of the sizeable black wolf stalking alongside me, unwilling to leave my side. Sten, as I called him, had been a trusted companion for years, traveling with me everywhere. As tended to be his way when visiting others, he sat outside Bjǫrn's lodge and kept guard once we went inside.

After accepting a horn of ale from a servant, I joined them around an inviting fire, noting the way Bjǫrn scowled and shook his head sharply at Freya when she tried to help him sit. Instead, he waved her away, grunting and wincing while lowering into his chair.

"You offended me by not accepting my daughter's gifts, Soren," Bjǫrn led out. His gaze narrowed on me, and he shook his head. "And in front of my people, no less. That alone gives me grounds to reject this marital pact."

"It does," I agreed, glancing from Freya, who sat beside her father, resting a hand possessively on her shield, and then back to Bjǫrn. "Yet 'twas my intention as Freya's future husband to honor her above all others." I lowered my head in respect to Bjǫrn, then lifted my chin to meet his eyes, praying I spoke to the man I once knew. "Forgive me if I offended you, but 'tis my fondest hope Freya only ever holds me in the highest regard, as I have long held such esteem for her." Glancing from her shield and blade back to Bjǫrn, I arched my eyebrows. "So, I would have it that she keeps her prized weapons, for did you not raise her to be a shield-maiden?"

"I did," Bjǫrn conceded, his brow caught in a never-ending furrow of distress and perhaps disappointment. "Yet I don't want her battling lest there's no choice. I want her to start a new lineage that combines the power of the bear and the wolf. A lineage that will ensure a lasting kinship betwixt our people, well into the future." He tossed back a swig of ale and gestured at Freya. "She is young and fertile, destined to lay down her shield and bear strong sons." Shaking his head, his voice grew especially gruff. "'Tis the only way I will agree to this."

Freya protested, "Despite raising me as a shield-maiden after my mother's death so that I might—"

"Lay down your shield when 'tis asked of you by your father." Bjǫrn cut her off, his eyes ablaze when they shot her way. "Lay down your shield so that you might wield a power far greater. One that will protect you and our kin far better than any shield ever could. Sons who will carry us forward into an ever-changing, unpredictable future."

"Mayhap we can find some middle ground here," I countered before Freya bit back with whatever she was about to say. "Mayhap, for the sake of what you wish all to see, we might try again during the celebrations this eve and have Freya gift her weapons to me. Then, I will return them to her at a later date, yet always do my best to keep her free of battle for I, too, want strong sons to carry on our lineage."

Just as I wanted all it took in bed to make those sons. Yet I forced myself to set aside those thoughts for now lest the image of her body free of clothing drive me to distraction.

"Nay," Bjǫrn returned, stubborn to the bone. "I would have Freya do as I asked from the beginning. Give you her weaponry for all to see, marking a new beginning betwixt our people." He shook his head. "You will *not* return them to her, even if there comes a time she must battle, which I would look unfavorably upon, but understand the choice is sometimes out of our hands." He gestured loosely at his daughter without glancing her way. "In that case, you may provide her with any other weapons with which to defend herself."

In truth, once Freya and I were married and she was mine, there was little Bjǫrn could do if I decided to return them to her. Yet I was a man of my word, so my stomach sank as that would not change even now. Not for her or anyone else. If I agreed to this, it would be my honor at stake, and nothing was more important. Frustratingly, it seemed that while I would have Freya in my bed, I suspected her heart might never belong to me because of this.

Yet there was no way around this. No counterargument would suffice. Bjǫrn refused to entertain anything but his wishes. So, I had no choice but to relent, hoping I might find another way to win her over once we were married.

"Are you sure about this, Bjǫrn?" I asked one more time, hoping I might at last appeal to him. "I recall how happy you were when gifting them to her. I witnessed it firsthand when I was younger." Still recalling the pleasure on his and his wife's faces at the time, I looked from Freya back to him. "Gifts from you and her mother, with your blessing, that she battled well with them and made you both proud."

"*Late* wife, and you would do well to remember it," Bjǫrn bit out, then downed half his ale in one long swig. "And Freya *has* battled well with them up until now, but no more." He shook his head once and looked me straight in the eyes. "Now she will hand them over and carry on our legacy with or without you, Soren. 'Tis the final time I will say it before I rescind this marriage pact."

Not about to let her go now that I nearly had her, there was no choice but to relent at last, despite Freya's ever-darkening expression. No choice but to nod and agree to Bjǫrn's wishes, however foolish I thought them. "I accept your terms, Bjǫrn Helvig, and will allow all to witness it this eve."

Even though Freya muttered under her breath in dismay, she quieted at the fierce scowl Bjǫrn aimed her way. Looking at me again, he raised his horn. "Then here is to a bright future full of strong sons born of the wolf and the bear."

I raised my horn in return. "To many strong sons."

Fully aware of Freya's rising tension, I downed the bitter ale in one long swig and nodded once at Bjǫrn, assuring him things would go as he wished from here on out.

After that, Bjǫrn asked a servant to summon Knud and ordered Freya to see me to my lodgings so that I might bathe and prepare for the evening's festivities. While he made it sound as if he needed to discuss preparations, I suspected he'd requested Knud to help him stand, as it was clear he struggled. While tempted to offer my assistance, I knew better. To his way of thinking, it would only make him appear weak.

So, I followed Freya out, aware she was displeased for a couple of reasons. Not only did things not go her way, but her father had asked her to escort me, which would have been a more appropriate task for a servant. Or so I assumed, based on her mutterings. She was by no means subtle in her musings while leading me and my wolf down a path cutting between cottages.

"Can you not speak to me directly, Freya?" I asked, eager to hear her lovely voice without venom on her tongue. "Were we not once friends?"

She stopped and frowned at me, her gaze fierce, only highlighted by her war paint. "Friends?"

"*Ja*, friends," I reiterated, wondering at the confusion on her face. "Do we not share childhood memories and a friendship? For I thought highly of you when our fathers visited."

"We were allies." She shook her head. "Nothing more." Her fiery amber eyes narrowed. "And that will remain true going forward because you're no true warrior, relenting to my feeble father so swiftly." Her gaze swept over me with disdain. "No warrior I will ever admire, given how little argument you possessed when fighting such an important battle."

Biting back both amusement and frustration, I arched an eyebrow at Sten when she strode on without a backward glance. "Is she not just as feisty as I told you she would be, my friend?"

Sten perked his ears forward, eyed me, and trudged after her, when typically he would remain by my side, telling me he was as intrigued by her as I was. Meanwhile, she slowed and glanced back as though curious about the way I had just spoken to my wolf. Then she stopped at a sizeable lodge not all that far from Bjǫrn's, meant for esteemed guests. So said the well-furnished interior when she opened the door and gestured for me to enter, where several servants awaited me.

"They will see to you," she said bluntly, then strode away from the lodge before I could say another word.

And so, they did, and quite well, both women attractive and attentive whilst bathing me and seeing me dressed. While neither did anything of the sexual variety, I sensed they were willing by their coy, appreciative glances and caressing touches while grooming me.

Yet they were not Freya, nor did their touches feel like I imagined hers might. Though soft, their skin didn't feel as silky. Though gentle, they weren't tender. And while both of them were lovely, neither was half as beautiful as Freya, nor nearly as fierce. Some men might prefer that, but I wasn't one of them. The fire in her eyes had always drawn me. The ferociousness simmering within, that might only ever soften for me.

That might only ever allow me to see what lies beyond.

There was so much more to Freya than she showed the world, and I wanted to be part of it. To see past her walls to the passionate woman beneath. To know all she held close to her heart, because I sensed it was vast. *She* was vast in ways most could not see. Though I was unsure of why I felt such, I did.

Eventually, I joined my men in the great lodge where celebrations were well underway. Several fires burned in pits down the center of the building, and flames sizzled in hanging bowls as flutes played, drums beat, and people ate, drank, danced, and laughed. The air smelled of smoke, spices, and succulent meat, and all seemed in good spirits.

Soon after I finished sharing an ale with my men, Bjǫrn entered with Freya and summoned me to join them at the head table. I found it difficult looking anywhere but at her in her finery, undoubtedly appearing the way her father might have wished it upon my arrival. Free of its braids now, her glorious auburn locks flowed softly around her shoulders, and her war paint was gone.

Instead, she had subtly highlighted her delicate features and lined her luminous, thickly lashed, almond-shaped eyes with coal. Her heart-shaped lips were pink and plush, making me long to feel them beneath mine. To finally kiss her as I had long dreamt. At last, to pull her close and taste her.

Before sitting, Bjǫrn spoke, and a hush fell over the crowd despite his weakened voice. He still had a way of commanding or, at least, a level of respect, that made his people take heed.

"'Tis our great honor to welcome the now infamous Earl Soren Dahl, 'The Brazon', into our tribe." He grasped my shoulder and gestured at Freya. "Soon to be married to my daughter, Freya, at last bringing together the wolf and the bear, uniting both tribes in greatness far into the future."

The crowd roared in approval before quieting at Bjǫrn's gesture to be silent, then seemed to wait, just as I did, with bated breath as Freya stepped forward. She gripped her weapons so tightly her knuckles whitened, and defiance flared in her gaze.

Could she ultimately do this?

Would she be able to see through her father's wishes?

We soon found out.

CHAPTER THREE

Freya

I WAS *FURIOUS*.

Unwaveringly, ferociously, *furious*.

How else could it be when Soren had so easily given in to my father's ridiculous wishes that I hand over my prized weapons and vow to do nothing but bear my husband strong sons upon our marriage? In retrospect, I couldn't help but wonder if Soren ever truly intended to counter my father in the end, however much he might have initially seemed opposed.

Now here I was in the great lodge, having had no choice but to dress as my father wished under my sister's close supervision, getting ready to do as he asked. No small task, but again, what choice did I have as my father, Knud, and Tove stood close, daring me to do otherwise? Not just that, but my talisman warmed again, telling me I was on the right path.

So, however much I disliked it, I approached Soren, blade and shield in hand, and stopped before him. Though I tried to keep the compliant, submissive expression my father longed to see, it was impossible as I met Soren's eyes. Instead, he saw only what I would offer my opponent in battle while handing over my weapons, dutifully saying all the words my father wanted to hear.

This time, however, Soren didn't reject my offerings but

willingly accepted them, seeming to tear away all that made me who I was in one fell swoop.

"'Tis a most humble gesture, Freya Helvig," he rumbled, saying words he need not say. "I will cherish these always." His voice rose so that all could hear. "Might we someday share them not just with strong sons, but strong daughters born of wolf and bear alike?"

Even though my father grumbled something under his breath about leaving daughters out of this, Soren's words earned another roar of approval from the crowd. After that, Bjørn insisted that everyone enjoy the fine fare of seasoned herring, succulent meats, seasoned vegetables, and freshly baked bread with warm honey as we sat at the head table with Tove and Knud on one side of Father and me and Soren on the other.

As it had been since meeting Soren, and despite my dislike of his relenting to my father, I remained overly aware of him by my side. Far too aware of his sheer size and masculine scent. A warm, delicious, heady combination of spice and pine that made it hard to focus on any other aroma.

Yet, I needed to after the day's events, so I tried my best to focus elsewhere. While a part of me understood that my father would never budge on his request, I had hoped Soren truly meant what he had said. That he would find some clever way to get through to Bjørn.

"'Tis fine fair," Soren complimented my father. He looked from my plate to me, as blunt now as he had been earlier when wondering if we were still friends. "Are you so angry with me that you won't enjoy your food? If I recall correctly, you once loved this type of fish."

He was right. I did. And it irked me that he remembered because it again spoke to his apparent affection for me when we were younger. Indeed, most women would be flattered or at least think more favorably about the union, but I wasn't most women. I was a shield-maiden forced into a marriage where my worth would lie solely in my breeding abilities rather than my battle skills.

"I believe you also favored sweets above all others," he went on, seemingly unfazed by my cold reception. A small smile curled his mouth. "To the point, you refused to allow me to have any after we snuck some from the kitchens one afternoon."

A good memory to be sure, and enough to invoke a response because he wasn't recalling it correctly.

"I tried to give you some, but you refused," I reminded. "So, I gave your share to pigs."

"And why did I refuse?" he prompted, amusement still twinkling in his eyes. He leaned closer and lowered his voice. "Surely you remember, Freya."

My breath caught at his proximity, and I struggled to speak for a moment before finally finding my tongue, remaining vague because I *did* recall. "As I said, you decided against your share, so I gave it to the pigs."

"You lie," he said softly, close enough that I felt his warm breath fan across my cheek. He assessed me in a way that made my heart beat a little harder. Almost as if he could see inside me, but of course, he could not. If anything, he excelled at observing others despite my guarded expression.

"I gave you my share because I knew you favored it and wanted you to enjoy it," he continued. "I would have given you anything when we were children, just as I intend to once you become my wife."

"Then give me back my shield and dagger," I countered, making the mistake of turning my head and looking into his eyes while so close. I meant to say more but struggled to find the words. Or the very thoughts that led to the words. Instead, I felt trapped in his piercing, stormy, blue-gray gaze. Held captive in a way that made thinking impossible.

"No," he murmured, seeming just as caught in my eyes. "But I'll give you any other shield and dagger you like because I won't have you defenseless." He shook his head. "Not ever."

Although tempted to rebuke him again because I was frustrated, I was also not blind to how genuine he seemed, nor that he could refuse me weaponry once we wed if he so chose. In days of old, women had more say, but times were changing, and with the spread of the new religion and a reduced need for women to fight, Norsemen, like most men, were slowly gaining more power over their female counterparts.

"Then I would have you give me weaponry the moment we set sail on the morrow," I said, testing him.

"The moment we are out of your father's sight," he vowed, most serious. "You have my word."

Feeling my talisman warm and seeing the truth in his eyes, I let the matter drop, lest my father overhear. Rather, I decided this might be a good opportunity to understand what it would be like living among his people. To prepare myself for a new life away from everything I knew and everyone I loved. While Soren might consider us friends and hold me in esteem, our childhood seemed a lifetime ago, and my memories of his stronghold were sparse. In fact, the only time I was there, I fell ill, so I recalled very little.

"Tell me what will be expected of me after we wed," I said rather than asked, sipping my ale, my tone dry. "Other than bearing you strong sons."

"And strong daughters," he reminded, his voice gentle if not rather husky with emotion, almost as if the thought of it truly appealed to him. "Preferably ones with the same strength and courage of their mother." He cleared his throat and sipped his ale. "But hopefully none so beautiful as I know well the thoughts of men."

The same intense heat from earlier burned beneath my skin when he looked at me with unmistakable appreciation, if not outright desire. I had seen that look in men's gazes before, but it never made me feel like this. Did he have this effect on all women? Apparently, those who had bathed him and attended to his needs were gossiping and blushing over his fine form. Yet despite their attempts to stimulate him, he made no move to return their affections, whereas many men might have, whether marrying soon or not.

I know because I had dealt with it firsthand years ago, despite not having invited it. Dealt with an attack that made me fear lying with men. None had ever made me feel less fearful and more responsive until Soren.

"So you will teach our daughters to battle?" I managed, praying my cheeks didn't warm as much as the rest of me, and gave him the wrong idea, even though I suspected it was very much the right idea.

"*We* will teach our daughters," he corrected. "As we will teach our sons." His eyebrows swept up. "For are you not a renowned shield-maiden in your own right, Freya? I might have relented to your father, but I meant what I said on the shore and wish this arrangement could be otherwise."

"Then why not persist?" I returned, trying my best not to be charmed by him. He had clearly developed not just physically but in the ways of flirting with the opposite sex. Frowning, I spoke out of genuine curiosity rather than anger and frustration. "Why didn't you fight harder? Why give in to his wishes so easily?"

"Because this is a truly favorable arrangement for our country," he replied logically. His voice turned husky again, and his gaze lingered on my face. "And because I would not risk losing you again."

It seemed he was about to say something else, but after his attention flickered from my father back to me, he thought better of it, and he shook his head. "It matters not." Catching me off guard, he lightly fingered a lock of my hair, as if he had been longing to do it for years. "What matters is I want you now and was willing to do whatever it took to get you."

I inhaled sharply at the feel of his warm fingers brushing the side of my neck before he pulled away when my father summoned forth our tribe's bard to sing tales of old. Stories that spoke of our people and the great polar bear spirit that watched over and fought alongside us. A means to impress Soren and his men so that they might regale their people with tales of what their chieftain's new bride brought to the clan. The great strength

I would lend them through our children.

Yet all the while, I remained aware of Soren by my side and hardly heard the tales. I thought about the things he had said and the way he said them. The emotion and intensity in his words. I thought about the stories I had heard of his escapades and of the scrawny boy he'd once been. More so, I reflected on the friend he had once been, because even though I wouldn't admit it, I *did* remember our moments together.

What had he meant by not losing me *again*? I knew nothing of that because we had made no promises to each other when we were young. There was no love beyond friendship. Perhaps some infatuation, to his childhood way of thinking, as he did take up his wooden sword when he thought me in harm's way, but that was it. Nothing more.

We had little chance to talk again after that, despite my hoping we would, because I wanted to understand what I might expect in the coming days. Soren spent most of his time with my father and their men, discussing what the unification of our tribes would mean for the future. Perhaps there would be more marital ties to bind us? Trade deals? Battles we would fight together if the king called upon us?

Yet all the while I was aware of the way Soren caught my eye every so often as if wanting me to know he would much rather be talking to me. So said the warming of my talisman yet again, forever steering me toward my destiny.

Our destiny.

"Come, sister," Tove said later in the evening, falling in beside me in a merry crowd that seemed determined to separate me and Soren with a thick wall of warm bodies. A crowd I should be grateful for, but felt frustrated by as the evening wore on.

"We must ready you for the morrow as you will be leaving at sunrise," Tove went on.

I was surprised she would be assisting me, as my father rarely wanted her anywhere but by his and Knud's side. That's when I realized Soren had managed to capture both my father and

Knud's attention with ale and tales of his own tribe, giving Tove this opportunity. And though it might have been my imagination, when his gaze connected with mine across the room, and flickered from Tove to me, I got the impression he wanted me to take this time with my sister while we could.

Tove led me out without another word into the cold, blustery spring night, past the flickering torches to the dimly lit paths beyond. The chilled air smelled of an incoming storm, heavy fog drifts swirled around us, and wind gusted much like it had years ago when we first came across the gray wolf pup. Sensing something rather than seeing anything, I stopped and looked back to catch my wolf's eyes glinting through the fog.

"Do you see it, Tove?" I asked because neither she nor Astrid had after that first time. "'Tis our gray wolf."

"Nay," Tove said, slowly unsheathing her blade when a sizeable black wolf emerged from the fog behind us. "'Tis Soren's and I will not hesitate to cut down the beast if he comes any closer."

"'Tis alright," I said softly when the wolf stopped and our gazes locked. "He's not going to hurt us, sister."

"How can you be so sure?"

"Because his hackles are down," I reasoned, despite sensing it more than anything when my talisman once again warmed. "If he meant to attack, he would bare his fangs and raise his hackles."

"Even so, 'tis rumored he never leaves his master's side, so why is he here?" Tove kept her blade in hand. "'Tis said he rarely strays from Soren's side unless he's protecting the entrance of wherever he goes."

"Then we must assume he feels his master is safe within our tribe," I replied. "And that mayhap he is choosing to watch over us at the moment."

Or me, I thought, certain I was right and unsure what to make of that.

I continued heading for my cottage, urging Tove to do the same, yet all the while I wondered at the wolf's appearance. Why did he follow me? Because I knew he did. Just as I knew that my gray wolf never strayed far, always watching me from the shadows.

Fortunately, Tove followed me into my cottage, glancing back one last time before shutting the door. "If I didn't know better, Soren commands the wolf every bit as much as we do the polar bear."

"You mean as *you* control the polar bear," I reminded, more pleased than I let on that she spoke to me like she once had. A sister rather than an overseer of my and Astrid's every move at our father's behest. To that end, I spoke plainly. "I'm surprised you are here, Tove."

"As am I," she conceded, surprising me yet again with her revelation. "'Tis your soon-to-be husband you should thank for that." She sheathed her blade and gestured at a pitcher of ale and two wooden cups left by a servant. "He insisted I be the one to see to your preparations so that we might have these last moments together as sisters, and shockingly enough, Father agreed." She gave an approving nod. "But then 'tis clear Soren has not just a way with blades but with words."

"It certainly seems that way," I said softly, adding wood to the dwindling flames on my hearth, more grateful to him for this time with my sister than he knew. Then again, perhaps he knew more than I gave him credit for. I looked her way. "Might we sit before the fire and talk as we once did over an ale or two? It has been too long, and I fear we may never again."

"As do I," she said, honest in a way I appreciated. She filled the cups, set them on a small wooden table nestled between two chairs before the fire, and sat. "So let us catch up whilst we can, then do as we have done with Astrid since her departure."

"*Ja*," I murmured, knowing what she meant without her saying so.

Although we had exchanged rare letters over the past year, it was our talismans that helped us understand each other from afar, in the way of the seers. Occasionally, it was just a feeling, and other times a sign, oftentimes through the flames of fire, such as the one we sat in front of now. We always knew it was her from the distant shores of Scotland, and she knew it was us.

"I miss her," Tove murmured. "Just as I will miss you."

"And I you, sister." I looked her way. "But I will always be with you, just as Astrid will always be with us. Just as your bear is with you, my wolf is with me, and her huskies with her. Our protectors, all."

She smiled at the reminder of the litter of wolf-like dogs Astrid had found at the Russian border before heading south years ago. The natives had called them *huskies*, and Astrid continued calling them that when they took to her and traveled with us when we relocated.

Enjoying ourselves, Tove and I talked for hours, just as we had in the past. She even laughed for the first time in years, and so did I, warmed by a camaraderie I'd thought lost to us. Though she might have embraced me yesterday, I had started to wonder if the strong bond we once shared still existed. Yet it seemed it did as we retold stories of our youth, careful to avoid talking about our future, for it would only ever pull us apart.

"He cares for you," Tove eventually murmured, her tongue loosened by the ale. She gazed into the flames. "He always has."

"Who?" I wondered.

"You know who." And I did, though I was reluctant to admit it. She met my eyes. "Since we were children, he saw you, but you did not see him. Now you do, though. Now—"

She was about to say more, but a rap came at the door, and she was summoned away. Not before she embraced me one last time and looked at me with the wisdom of a big sister. "Stand strong, as you always have, Freya, and never hesitate to follow the path laid for you." She squeezed my shoulder, and rare emotion flickered in her gaze. "Follow your shield-maiden spirit, whether your shield is in hand or not." She pressed her hand to my heart. "For it is forever right here, warrior."

Before I could respond, she was gone into the night, with fog curling around her. As I stood in the doorway, I caught the eyes of Soren's wolf staring back as though he had been there all along, perhaps watching over me, before he faded into the fog as well.

That night, I dreamt only of the sea and a man with his wolf. Of saying goodbye to all I knew and setting out on a new journey. A dream that would, like many of them, soon come to pass...and little did I know just how turbulent that journey would end up being.

CHAPTER FOUR

Soren

THOUGH I SLEPT little that night after Freya left Bjǫrn's great lodge with her sister to prepare for leaving today, when I managed to rest, I dreamt only of Freya, hardly believing the day had finally come that she would go home with me.

That she would soon become my wife.

I dreamt of her finally smiling at me like she had when we were children. Of her wrapped in my arms as she was now, our limbs tangled when I pressed deep inside her. I would hear her soft moans of pleasure time and time again, because I would make it good for her every time. Ensure she only felt bliss when I made her mine as often as she allowed it. Not only because I longed to see her belly swell with our children, but also because I wanted her to find happiness in my arms.

Eager to set out, I rose early and made my way alongside my wolf down to the shore before my men rose, somehow not surprised to find Freya standing at the end of one of the piers gazing out at the distant storm. She had wrapped her hair in intricate braids for travel, and her white-fur bear cloak billowed around her.

Glad to find her here so that we might share this time alone, I joined her. "I see you still rise early."

"*Ja.*" She glanced from me back to the black-bellied clouds flickering with lightning. "It seems you still do as well."

I could not help a small smile that she recalled more of our time together than she'd admitted to yesterday. "So you *do* remember our time together as children."

She arched a delicate eyebrow at me. "Was that not clear last night when we spoke of sweets and pigs?"

"'Twas clear you remembered your version of events," I reminded, amused. "'Tis good you recall some things more clearly, as I enjoyed our morns together."

"I said I recalled you were an early riser," she countered. "Not that I remembered time spent together during those mornings."

"Somehow I don't believe you," I said softly, noting the way her cheeks had taken on a rosy hue. It was windy, but something told me her blush had nothing to do with the elements. "And I cannot help but wonder why you're so determined to make me think you forgot." I cocked my head. "Unless, that is, you fear I might take that for returned affection all those years ago. That perhaps you might not be as opposed to our upcoming nuptials as you have led me to believe."

"I never said I took issue with marrying you, Soren." She cut me a sharp look. "I took issue with you agreeing to take my prized weapons." Her gaze returned to the sea. "That aside, I'm thankful you found a way to distract Father and Knud last night so that Tove and I had time alone together." Emotion churned in her steady amber gaze. "'Twas truly appreciated."

"No need to thank me," I murmured, eyeing her lovely profile, thinking back on days of old. "I remember how close you once were with your sisters, so 'twas the least I could do for accepting your dagger and shield."

"And what of your wolf?" Her gaze slid to Sten, who sat by my side, taking in the scent of the sea. "Did you somehow order him to follow me last night as well?"

"Order Sten?" I chuckled. "He's wild, Freya. I could not order him to do anything. He does as he likes."

"Yet you named him as if you tamed him." She looked from Sten to me. "And he follows you. Protects you." Her brow furrowed. "He does this without any commands?"

"He does," I confirmed. "Since he was a pup, so 'tis good, if not telling, that he watched over you as well."

She hesitated, as if weighing whether to ask before relenting. "Telling how?"

"Telling because he's never looked after another until you," I revealed, my gaze lingering on her face because it felt impossible to look away. Impossible to see anything but her. "So I would say he finds you as worthy of protection as he does me." I brushed the pad of my thumb over her soft cheek before I could stop myself, pleased when she didn't pull away. "'Tis no small thing to earn that level of devotion from any wolf, let alone Sten, as his is an alpha's nature." I pulled my hand away but kept my gaze with hers. "But then you have always been of the wolf despite being born to a bear, have you not, Freya Helvig?"

"I have." Her voice sounded a bit breathless. "And well you know it, Soren Dahl."

"*Ja.*" My gaze dropped to the blue runic stone hanging around her neck. "I remember well the tale you spun of how you came into your stone and the gray wolf that watched over you afterward." I looked into her eyes again. "I thought it whimsical then, surely a story spun to gain my attention, for 'twas too unbelievable, but now I wonder. Was the wolf pup leading you to me somehow? Am I your destiny, as you claimed the stone would someday show you?"

Her pupils flared, and her gaze remained locked with mine before she looked to the sea and distant storm again. "You are the direction of the stone."

She was about to say more, but hesitated when we heard footfalls behind us and several of my men moved by, headed toward my ships, getting ready to prepare for travel.

"We should help them," Freya said when I knew she meant to say something else. Her eyes were lit with the first real flicker of excitement I had seen since coming together the day before. "I would like to help them. See your impressive boats firsthand and get a feel for them, as the way will be choppy at the very least."

"'Twill." Taking in the sky, I gauged the moody storm churning in the distance. "We will ride the coast down to my stronghold, but that storm will very likely move inland, so 'twill be rough on the water."

"Yet you don't want to remain here and let it pass," she noted, the sense of anticipation in her eyes warring with her nostalgia at leaving.

As always, Freya enjoyed the sea, no matter how rough. The danger and excitement it could offer. Though I had only ever been on a boat a few times with her in our youth, I saw clearly how sailing freed her spirit. And the rougher the seas, the freer she'd felt.

"No, I don't want to linger here a moment longer," I conceded. "I want to see you upon the seas once more, as it seems the gods intend to give you the kind of weather you most enjoy." I kept my gaze on her face a moment longer. "And whilst I know you love your people and the wilds of this isle, I would see you flourish beyond its shores as the friend I have long missed and my wife by nightfall, given preparations have already been made for your arrival." I nodded once to her. "So I will see you aboard soon, as my ships will soon be yours, Freya. My warriors, your warriors."

It was more than most men would give women these days, but I, though still young, had an older mindset and wanted her by my side, as she always should have been. Strong if not fierce. A true shield-maiden sent by the gods because I'd long thought she was, and loathed seeing her as anything else. I would have her know it, too. Mayhap not here with her father's eyes watching her every move, but someday. Someday soon.

So, I strode back down the dock to help my men, pleased when she fell in beside me, given I had long considered it her rightful place. Not only as the woman I desired above all others, but a steadfast companion who could fight as well as any man, or so I'd heard and did not doubt.

We said little to each other after I introduced her once more to those already preparing to travel, but then words were unnecessary. She took matters into her own hands and went from ship to ship, learning each one. Either with a question here or there to those aboard or by touching the wood and looking over the lines of each vessel with a keen eye. Yet always, I saw her glancing at the sea and weather, gauging as I was, the best course as it would prove tricky today.

Eventually, Tove, Knud, and Bjǫrn made their way down, along with several of Bjǫrn's men bearing gifts to honor our union. A wary look simmered on Bjǫrn's face that didn't surprise me or Freya, it seemed, as we met him on the pier.

"'Twill be dangerous weather for traveling." Bjǫrn frowned at the rumbling black clouds in the distance before turning his scowl my way. "You should stay another night and enjoy our hospitality. We have ample food and shelter."

"If we leave now, we will be fine," I assured, hoping I was right, yet my desperation to leave these shores with Freya outweighed all.

"*Ja*." Freya sounded just as eager, yet I feared not for the same reasons. "And few sail as well as I, nor know the weather like I do, so I can say, without doubt, Soren is right."

When Bjǫrn frowned and shook his head, displeased, Tove spoke, clearly surprising Freya. "They are right, Father." She looked up and considered the skies. "If they leave now, all will be well, and they will soon be married, tying the wolf and bear together by nightfall."

If that were not surprising enough, when Bjǫrn's brow furrowed in doubt and he kept shaking his head, his man, Knud, spoke, albeit gruffly, after Tove shot him a look I couldn't quite decipher. "Tove speaks the truth, chieftain. There is time if they catch the wind and move swiftly." His gaze swept over my boats. "These are fine ships that will cut through waves well manned by admirable sailors." He nodded once at me. "By an admirable chieftain."

"And an admirable Helvig," I added, looking from Freya to Bjǫrn. "If rumor holds true, few fare as well as your daughter on the sea."

Where I thought perhaps Freya would remain quiet because she'd clearly tested her limits with her father the day before, she did not, and once again, it worked in my favor.

""Tis true, Father." Freya pulled her shoulders back and looked Bjǫrn in the eyes. "None fares as well as I on the seas, no matter how turbulent, and well you know it. So trust in this journey, for if I don't aid us in safe travels, the gods surely will." Fingering the stone around her neck, she gestured at the land. "And if it becomes unsafe, know that my mother and your beloved wife, as she always has from the afterlife, will lead us to ground where we'll wait out the storm."

Seeming affected by those words above all, Bjǫrn's gaze lingered on her stone before he looked Freya in the eyes again. *"Ja?"*

"Ja," Freya assured, saying no more as they gazed at one another for a long moment before, thankfully, Bjǫrn nodded once.

"Then you best set sail soon," Bjǫrn said, his voice rough with emotion as he looked at his daughter before turning his attention my way. "I won't weigh your boats down much this day, as you must travel swiftly, but more is coming soon to bless you and Freya's union. Today, bear furs to warm your tribe and the two of you on your wedding night, and several freshly forged blades, may they protect you and yours always."

"As will our wolf furs until we can send more goods," I vowed, referring to the trunks of furs unloaded the previous evening. "May they keep you as strong and stealthy as the wolf in battle."

After that, we set to making final preparations and said our goodbyes within the hour. Although Bjǫrn did not embrace Freya, I didn't miss the emotion in his gaze when he told her to fare well and bear many strong sons. Her sister didn't embrace her either, yet she did press something into her hand and exchanged the fondest look I had seen on Tove's face thus far.

By the time we set out, the storm was closer and the seas rougher, much to Freya's delight. Or so it seemed, given that the sadness on her face while watching her sister and village fade into the distance was soon replaced with anticipation as she set to helping us navigate.

"It sails well," she praised at one point, looking over my ship with appreciation as it sliced through the choppy water. "You must have a fine boat builder."

"Brynhild is," I agreed.

Freya's eyebrows swept up. "She's a woman?"

"She is," I confirmed. "And has long overseen the building of Dahl ships."

"They are impressive, indeed." Freya ran her hand along the boat's smooth oak. "I look forward to meeting her."

"And she you."

A flicker of surprise lit her eyes. "She knows of me, then?"

"My entire tribe knows of you, Freya," I replied, taken with how she appeared on the sea, her hair vividly red and her amber gaze golden against the frothing dark greens and blues of the water. How suited she was to it, keeping her balance with ease despite the swaying boat. "Some remember you from when you visited as a child, and others have heard of your battling. Others still, your seer abilities. 'Tis not every day one comes across a shield-maiden who possesses such gifts."

"Gifts I rarely use nowadays," she warned, troubled where moments before her lovely face had been full of excitement. "'Tis important you understand that and make it clear to your people. I do not divine for anyone." She shook her head. "Not anymore."

While curious, we unfortunately had to focus on sailing rather than talking because the weather worsened. Though the skies darkened, thunder cracked, and rain fell, the shadows that had fallen over Freya's face at our discussion lifted, and excitement once again sparkled in her eyes. She clearly relished the ruthless sea, gusty winds, and the challenge of keeping afloat. While some manned the rudder, others rowed while Freya, I, and a few others worked the sails.

"We may have no choice but to go ashore soon, Soren," one of my men roared above the elements when it became impossible to speak normally.

He was right. We would soon be unable to make it past the breakers to go ashore. Truth told, it might already be too late.

"There's still time," Freya yelled over the booming thunder. As drenched as the rest of us, her wet hair was plastered to her head and her fur cloak sodden, yet she appeared unfazed when she looked at me and shook her head. "The winds are shifting to the south. Row hard away from the shore and then let the sails do more of the work than the oarsmen. 'Tis a safer option than trying to navigate inland at this point. The waters are too unstable."

I looked from the skies to the slant of the rain to the height of the waves, gauging her accuracy. Though it *was* risky, she was right. We could do it, but we would need to act swiftly, so I gave the orders, and we headed away from the coast.

Grinning, she took up an oar, impressing my men with her willingness to go where she was needed and row just as hard as anyone else. Staying with the sail, I waved at the other ships to follow suit, and we continued braving the turbulent waters until the winds did just as she had predicted. Lifting most of our oars, we raised another sail only for the ship to lurch south, caught by sure winds that gave us good speed against the waves.

I could not help but smile when Freya tossed back her head and laughed, giving us a glimpse of the infamous Helvig berserker. And Odin above, she was glorious when she smiled. When she laughed, and the throaty sound carried on the wind, I joined in her laughter, because it felt good. Good to laugh with her, enjoying the wild ride every bit as much.

And it only got better from there…until she asked me the last thing I wanted to hear later that day. Something that I would undoubtedly struggle to heed.

CHAPTER FIVE

Freya

WHILE A PART of me had dreaded leaving my tribe, another part had never felt so free when Soren's ship departed and I watched my father fade into the distance. Though saddened to say goodbye to my sister, and sad for the father I had lost years ago, despite his mortal body still being here, there was relief in starting out on my own, even if married to another.

I wondered at the small wolf pendant my sister had pressed into my hand before I left, just as I was curious about the look on her face when she did so. Fingering it in my pocket, I knew it meant something, but I wasn't sure what. All I knew was that I had never seen it before, yet it was meant to be with me. Meant to remind me of something, but I couldn't recall what.

Pendants and leaving home aside, nothing felt more thrilling than setting sail into stormy weather and rough seas. This was my element, and I knew Soren saw that. Moreover, I knew he felt the same. We were one on the water, and I felt it poignantly when he laughed as I laughed. When our eyes met, the same heat that always seemed to burn beneath my skin at his gaze grew hotter, sharper, more exciting, even as the icy rain and frigid winds lashed me.

The heat came so intensely this time, along with an alarming ache between my thighs, that I asked something of him once we were free of the worst of the storm and sailing down the coast. Asked because I feared the inevitable and felt I could. He was proving to be someone I could reason with, and I sensed that there was little he wouldn't do to keep our friendship intact.

Or so I hoped.

When we were alone, toward the front of the ship, and others couldn't hear us over their chatter and the lap of the waves against the hull, I leaned close and spoke softly, overly aware of him but determined to keep him at bay for now. No easy task given how my heart raced the closer he was, but then had a man's eyes ever matched the stormy blue gray of the sea and skies as well as his? Had they ever drawn me in and excited me as much as the turbulent weather we had just navigated?

"As I said before, 'twas good of you to allow Tove and me time together last night, and you have my thanks," I said, careful with my words. "'Twas a kindly gesture after giving in to my father and accepting my weapons, so I can only hope you're willing to offer me another boon as a token of goodwill toward our rekindled friendship."

The corner of his mouth curled up in a becoming way that made a small dimple appear in his cheek. "So we *are* friends once again, *ja*?"

"I would like to think so," I replied smoothly, offering him a soft smile. "If you would like."

"I very much would." His crooked grin remained intact, but his gaze narrowed a tad, as if he didn't entirely trust where I might be leading him. "And what would this request be, my friend?"

"That you honor our renewed friendship by allowing me time after our nuptials to get to know you again."

"Of course," he replied. "'Twould be my pleasure to spend time with you after we're married so that we might enjoy the friendship we once shared."

"'Tis good to hear." Relieved, I clarified what that meant now that he had agreed, without going into the finer details. "'Tis more than most husbands might allow after marrying, and 'twill make our final union together less dreaded, to be sure."

His eyes narrowed again, and he tilted his head in question. "Our final union?"

"*Ja.*" I was sure to look humbled, if not a tad bashful, when neither came naturally to me. "Before I give you the strong sons you promised my father."

His eyebrows shot up in surprise, and the corners of his mouth slanted down. "Surely, you're not referring to lying together after we marry, sealing our bond as man and wife?"

"I was, so you can see why I'm so grateful you agreed to this." I offered him a tentative, hopeful smile that again did not come naturally to me, but I would do whatever it took. "It speaks highly of the marriage we will share." I cocked my head at his troubled expression, sure to appear worried. "You did mean what you said, *ja?*"

Based on his wariness, I thought he would go back on his word, but he surprised me, cornering me as swiftly as I had him.

"I did mean what I said," he finally replied, eyeing me with a bit too much cunning if I didn't know better. "Yet I feel, given this is more than any husband would allow, that I would have you do something for me in turn? Otherwise, I might have to reconsider, given my people will be watching closely, and as you can imagine, expect something of this truly advantageous union."

"What did you have in mind?" I wondered.

"That you allow my affections until you're ready to fulfill your marital obligations," he said. "'Tis more than fair to ask of you, and 'twill help quell any rumors of us not yet being properly betrothed."

"And what do you consider affections?" I countered, sensing there would be no way around this.

"Need you ask?"

"I would not have asked otherwise."

"Anything that gives the appearance of us being together as

we should," he returned. Despite his being as soaked as me in the chilly weather, the pad of his thumb felt warm against my cool cheek when he dusted it along my jaw. "Mayhap an embrace here or there, or the touch of my lips against yours. Your hand in mine or even just this as I feel your cheek. All signs of affection that would appease curious eyes."

Sensing he might change his mind about lying together if I disagreed, and knowing he was not entirely wrong in his request, I did the only thing I could and conceded to his stipulation. Yet as triumph flared in his gaze and he pulled away, leaving a trail of warmth where he'd touched me and a breathless sensation that had not been there before, I realized his affections might very well work against my wishes. His effect on me, whether standing close or touching me, was tangible if not outright arousing.

After that, we spoke of other things, namely what I could expect once we made landfall, but the discussion we'd had about intimacy lingered in my mind, and I worried. Although my virtue had remained intact after I was attacked years before, the fear of nearly losing it that night against my will still haunted me.

Given my own experience, I had never quite understood why women found pleasure in a man's arms, because I'd heard their lusty moans of pleasure within my own tribe, yet I was getting a better idea since Soren arrived. Now, it became increasingly challenging to think of anything but what it might feel like to feel the affection of which he spoke, never mind letting him between my thighs. More pointedly, I found myself eager for his next touch rather than dreading it.

He pointed out trunks full of shields, axes, and blades, seeing through his promise when he urged me to take whatever I liked now that we were out of my father's sight. And though I didn't mind my wet clothes in the cold wind, I was grateful when he replaced my wet bear fur with one of the few that had remained relatively dry in my trunk.

"Whilst some of the wolf furs remained drier," he murmured in my ear, removing my wet fur and wrapping the other around my shoulders from behind, "'Tis only right you return to my, *our*, people wearing the bear."

He didn't step away but remained close with his hands resting on my shoulders when we rounded the bend, and his stronghold appeared in the distance in all its glory. Easily double the size of my father's, and tucked between mountains steeped in clouds, it was well-fortified with an admirable wall, protecting the numerous longhouses and cottages within. If that were not impressive enough, his fleet of ships certainly was.

"Your boat builder, Brynhild, has been busy," I exclaimed, shocked that even now, with so much sprawling out in front of me, I could be more aware of his heat and touch at my back than this place I would soon call home.

"She has," he rumbled, his voice deeper than usual and still close to my ear. "What do you think of it all, Freya? Though you might not recall, much has changed since the last time you were here."

"It has," I agreed. "Though to be honest, 'tis a bit hazy as I suspect I was already coming down with a fever by the time I arrived."

"No doubt you were," he said, finally standing alongside me, but not before—I swore—he inhaled my scent as if he could not help himself. "You didn't look well upon arrival."

"I'm surprised you remember," I said. "'Twas years ago."

"I remember every time I saw you." His gaze grew shadowed when he looked at me. "Especially that time because you became gravely ill."

It was clear from the haunted look on his face that my state had troubled him greatly. Enough to speak once again to his esteem for me in our youth. Yet as his gaze lingered on my face, and my talisman warmed against my chest, I got the sense there was more to that visit than I recalled. Something he was not sharing. Before I could ask what, his focus returned to the shore, and he smiled as more and more people made their way onto the docks to greet us.

A towering giant of a man with an expression even darker than the one Knud usually wore greeted us once we lowered the sails, the ship was tied off, and we made our way onto the pier. If that is, one wanted to call the brute's simple nod and fierce scowl at me a greeting. Dressed much like Soren in a dark leather tunic and trousers, he wore a thick black fur over his shoulders, had shaved the sides of his light brown, braided hair, and woven several small braids into his beard.

Soren introduced him as his good friend and second-in-command, Ivar. The man he left in charge when he was not here.

"'Tis just a matter of Ivar getting to know you better," Soren said, after his man offered me nothing more than a grunt hello and went to oversee the unloading of the ships. "He's never taken well to outsiders. Once he trusts you, he will lay down his life for you, and few warriors are so fierce or loyal."

"Something tells me his trust is not easily won," I said, not put off by Ivar's cold greeting, but then curtness and grumpiness were something I was used to with my father.

"Ah, 'tis good to lay eyes on you again, my boy," a short, slender, older woman said boisterously, grinning from ear to ear as she strode for Soren with a slight gait and pulled him into a hearty embrace.

Clearly a force unto herself, the woman, with her intricately braided, white-streaked gray hair, turned one sharp blue eye my way as the other was hazed over with white, speaking to blindness, and kept smiling just as broadly. "And 'tis even better to see you looking so well, Freya Helvig. 'Tis far past time you returned to these shores once and for all."

"This is Brynhild, Freya," Soren said fondly. "Not just my boat builder, amongst other things, but my aunt. You likely do not remember, but Brynhild helped tend to you when you'd first arrived years ago and grew ill."

"I have no memory of that, but you have my heartfelt thanks, Brynhild." I returned her smile. "'Tis good to be back." Glancing from the ship on which we had arrived and back to her, I couldn't help but praise her. "Your ships are very well made. You are to be commended."

"'Tis less me these days building them but overseeing their construction, but thank you nonetheless." She gestured for me to join her. "Come. Let me show you around whilst Soren sees to his men, then ready you for the evening as 'twill be grand indeed."

When I looked at Soren, unsure if I should follow rather than assist with the ships, he insisted I go, so I did, at ease with Brynhild far faster than I was with most strangers. She had an inner strength and self-confidence that I appreciated. One that seemed to persevere despite her aging body.

As she led me past children playing at the shore and merchants selling goods at carts through the front gates, she described all the renovations and fortifications Soren had made to the stronghold since losing his father.

"And what of his mother?" I remembered her gentle ways and kind manner from when they visited us in my youth.

"My sister is no longer with us," Brynhild said softly. "Gone for years now but never forgotten." There seemed to be an all-knowing glint in her gaze when she looked at me. "You remember her fondly, do you not?"

"I do," I confessed. "So it saddens me to hear this."

"No doubt it does," she murmured before the shadows that had briefly settled around her eyes lifted, and she offered me a warm smile. "Today is not for sad memories, though, but to create good memories, is it not? Because I don't doubt my sister would want this day celebrated above all others."

"Would she, then?"

"*Ja*, to be sure." Brynhild pointed out various things along the way, such as the stables, weaponry, the smithy, and other important buildings. "For the bear finally weds the wolf, bringing great change and new beginnings."

My talisman marked the truth in her words when it warmed, telling me once again that I was on the right path. I swore the wolf pendant my sister had given me heated as well, but when I slipped my hand into my pocket, it was cool to the touch.

The deeper we walked into the village, the more scents permeated the air. Although I still caught the scent of sea salt on the wind, it now mixed with that of wood smoke and freshly baked bread. People smiled at me in passing before Brynhild led me into a cottage beside a sizeable lodge with a deeply sloping roof meant for someone of importance.

"This will be your cottage when you wish to use it," Brynhild enlightened upon entering the warm, inviting building. It hosted a bed with plush fur, a crackling fire, as well as a basin for bathing, and a small table holding a pitcher of ale and a variety of cheese and bread on which to snack. She asked the servant tending to things to bring warm water for bathing.

"I know this place," I said softly, feeling as if I had stepped into a dream. "How do I know this place?"

"You know it because you were here before, Freya," Brynhild said just as softly, helping me remove my fur cloak. "'Twas where you were tended when you fell ill."

"Whose cottage is it?" I wondered, feeling like I should know the answer. More than that, I felt it hovering somewhere in my mind and heart just out of reach, dusting my memory with hazy moments I couldn't quite grasp.

"Let me help you prepare for your wedding and I will share." Brynhild poured ale into a wooden cup and handed it to me, her gaze as kind now as I remember her sister's being so long ago. "You see, my sister was a healer, and she—"

"Healed me," I murmured, seeing a flash of kind eyes, the same dark blue gray of Soren's staring down at me. While caught in a memory, I felt her cool, soft hand against my blazing hot forehead. "Or at least, she tried…"

"Let us sit and enjoy a drink together whilst your bath is prepared," Brynhild urged, gesturing at a chair in front of the fire. "And I will tell you of when the wolf and bear first truly came together. 'Twas in this very cottage on an eve much like this one."

Curious what she meant, I sat and listened to a tale about a young boy and girl. Of Soren and me, in this cottage, many years ago.

"Like most you traveled with, you became gravely ill shortly after arriving," Brynhild said. "'Twas at young Soren's insistence that his mother see after you, though I suspect she would have anyway. Not just because you were the daughter of the bear and her son had begged it of her, but because she felt drawn to you in a way she couldn't put to words."

"But what of the others?" I wondered.

"She saw to them, too, but we had other healers, so she spent most of her time tending to your needs." Her gaze a touch sad, as if she looked back in time at those moments, she sipped her ale and stared into the flames. "You were but a child…far too young to go to the gods."

"And I did not." Sipping my ale, I was pleased by its smooth taste yet saddened by the conversation in a way I didn't quite understand. "Thanks to her, *ja*?" I frowned. "Though my parents never did share such, and for that I'm sorry."

"As am I, but then times were different back then," Brynhild said. "The wolf had yet to come into its full strength, and the bear had yet to be crippled. 'Twas a time of friendship but not marriage pacts."

There was no need to ask what she meant because I remembered my father before his injuries. How prized my sisters and I were, given the substantial accomplishments of our tribe under his earldom. To promise me or my sisters to any other tribe at the time would have been foolish had they not been as great as ours, and none were. Not until now.

Not until Soren had brought his earldom so very far.

"Soren's father tried to arrange a marriage betwixt us far sooner, didn't he?" I said softly, seeing things clearly enough now. "But my father rejected it."

Although about to respond, Brynhild paused when a soft rap came at the door, and she was summoned away before she could divulge more due to a problem with one of the ships only she could resolve. Yet I got the sense as she left and my stone warmed once more that her departure might have been more purposeful than an issue with a boat.

Soon after, my trunks arrived, followed by several servants to prepare my bath and help me get ready. All the while, I mulled over a past with this tribe that seemed hazy at best. I recalled well enough Soren visiting our tribe, but even then, they were the memories of youth, and those could so easily become warped in one's mind over time.

After bathing, I blinked back tears when I discovered our mother's marital dress in a trunk Tove had sent along. Not just that, but one of my father's swords, along with a family ring engraved with the Helvig bear insignia. While I would like to think my father had provided these to exchange with Soren during our matrimony, something told me he had not. He'd been too preoccupied with taking blades from me, not the other way around. Either way, I was grateful I had something to offer Soren, given our tribes still practiced the old ways born of our Viking ancestors.

Although I was still unsure why I hadn't grabbed a blade and shield when Soren offered them to me on his ship, the timing had not seemed right, and I couldn't say why. Especially considering I was a shield-maiden meeting my new tribe for the first time. Perhaps out of pride because they weren't my own? Yet some-how that didn't feel like the reason.

Curiosities aside, it was time to see through my fate.

So, once dressed and properly adorned, I was led back to the shore to marry, and my life started anew, taking me down roads I didn't know awaited me. However, interestingly enough, it turned out that, mayhap, Soren and his mother very much had.

CHAPTER SIX

Soren

"WHY DID YOU call me away, nephew?" Brynhild joined me on the pier after seeing Freya to her cottage, where I remained perplexed by what I saw. "Did you not want me to see to Freya's needs and prepare her for what was to come? Prepare her for stories of your youth that might soon greet her ears?"

Though Brynhild batted me away, prideful in her later years, I still helped her into a newly built boat that had yet to set sail and pointed out a crack in the wood at the front. While not an integral piece that should not affect the vessel's sailing abilities, I found it alarming, if not chilling, in its own way.

"Is that not the very crack that formed on the boat that carried Freya to our shores when I was a boy?" I frowned at her. "The very crack that formed as she battled illness?"

"It certainly seems it," Brynhild murmured, equally awed. She ran her fingers along strong, durable wood that should not crack like this. Wood she knew well from an oak tree she had hand-selected herself. "I neither possess the gifts of your mother nor of she who will soon be your wife, but I would say this is a sign." She looked to the horizon, then to me. "One of a divide to come once more."

"'Tis not what I want to hear." I frowned. "Not if it means to divide me and Freya yet again." Biting back emotion, I shook my head. "Not as it nearly did before. As it would have if not for my mother, may she forever dine by Odin's side in Valhalla."

"And I don't doubt she will because she was the greatest warrior," she said softly, resting a comforting hand on my arm. "One who fought battles you and I would never be capable of fighting, saving countless, not with a blade but with the gift that lay in her healing touch."

"*Ja*," I murmured, missing her but proud of her. "I'm sorry that I called you away from Freya's side on such an eve, but 'twas important you see this. Important that I knew this boat would be safe above all others."

"'Twill be," my aunt assured. "This crack is about prophecy rather than safety."

"Yet are they not often intertwined?" I reminded.

"When it comes to Freya, *ja*, but you need not fear that this boat will sink." She rested her hand on the hull. "'Tis a strong ship built for an equally strong shield-maiden." Curious, she slid me a look. "Might she someday soon hold a shield once again as she should?"

I had noticed Freya didn't end up taking anything from the trunks of weapons on our ship earlier, and could only hope it meant she didn't feel threatened.

"Aye, my aunt, she shall soon have another shield in hand if she wishes it," I promised, helping her back onto the dock despite her trying to bat me away again. Whether she liked it or not, her old bones needed assistance. Especially on such a cold, damp day. "'Twill not be the shield it should be, but *'twill* be a shield."

When she looked at me in question as we headed back to the village, I told her of everything that had happened among the Helvig tribe. Specifically, with Freya's father, Bjǫrn.

"'Tis a shame he went down such a path when once he let his daughters shine," she said in contemplation. "Yet you think it all out of fear for their safety? That he smothers them now rather than letting them be the strong daughters he raised them to be?"

"Make no mistake, they still are." I urged her to take my arm, not surprised when she waved me away once more and stuck to it this time. "But *ja*, in my opinion, he does not want them fighting but breeding, of the mind it will keep them safe."

"And what of the daughter he sent off to the wilds of Scotland?" she wondered with a knit brow. "Is she safe, given she is the youngest and, if I recall correctly, the least brazen of the three?"

"From what I heard, Astrid fares well enough and wields words as efficiently as she wields a blade these days," I replied. "She's skilled at the various dialects of the Scots, English, and Norse alike, so she is much valued."

"So, she has become a peacekeeper?" Brynhild exclaimed. "During such trying times, when last I heard, we Norse barely hold claim to the land of the Scots nowadays?" She shook her head. "That doesn't sound like something a father would approve of when he's so determined his daughters forfeit their shields for strong sons."

"Nay," I agreed. "But that's what I heard." Eyeing her pained gait and wanting her to rest, I looked at her in question. "Join me for an ale?"

"Nay, I will go ready myself for such an important eve." She stopped and looked at me with all the fondness my own mother once did. "An eve you have long awaited, and I couldn't be happier for you. This is meant to be in ways my sister saw long ago." She pressed her hand to my heart. "That *you* felt long ago, and now the gods have delivered you to each other as it always should have been."

"Thank you, Aunt." I rested my hand over hers, fearful to feel hope and happiness after seeing the crack on the boat. Yet the moment had arrived, so I set aside my trepidation for now. "I look forward to a night of celebration."

Passing Freya's cottage soon after, I wasn't surprised to see Sten standing guard outside her door. Even though I longed to go inside where she prepared for our nuptials, I held back and sighed, thinking about the promise I'd made not to lie with her tonight and make her my wife in every sense of the word. Granted, I had every intention of seducing her because I felt her reaction to me when we were close, yet still. It wasn't the same as knowing with certainty I would have her at long last this very eve.

Even so, she *would* become my wife soon and sleep within my lodge. It would be inappropriate for her to sleep elsewhere. I had not figured out the finer points of how that would work, but I put those thoughts from my mind for now and focused on preparing myself so that I might lay my eyes on her once more. It may seem like a small thing, but for me, seeing her, merely *being* near her, was all I truly wanted. Craved.

After bathing and dressing, I went to one of the trunks carried in earlier and pulled out her prized shield and blade, wishing I could return them to her tonight. They were hers and should be with her, but alas, I had promised Bjǫrn and would keep my word, so I saw them carefully stored elsewhere in my lodge. Somewhere they would not readily taunt her in hopes that she liked what I would replace them with.

Then, after grabbing a shield, sheathing a family blade, and pocketing a ring that meant a great deal to me, I made my way to the shore and joined Ivar, who stood stoically amid celebrations already underway. Drums beat and flutes tootled a merry jig, as people chatted, danced, and sang. Adorned with flowers, bones, talismans, and other trinkets for our matrimony, and back-dropped by a glittering moonlit sea, an archway flanked by torches awaited me and Freya. I could see my mother's shield placed behind it as I had requested.

"Must you look so dire, old friend?" I said to Ivar, grinning. After accepting a horn of ale, I smiled at my people as they smiled at me, happy to welcome the bear into our den, for it was Freya Helvig, and she was a legend in these parts.

"I will look any which way I want," Ivar grunted, forced to

accept a horn of ale too when I furrowed my brow at him and told him he'd better. "And I will do so until she proves her worth."

Though tempted to remind him that her worth was renowned beyond these walls and more so within them once she became my wife, I knew better than to have the same old argument with him. Not when he cast blame on her she knew nothing about, and didn't deserve. To his mind, she'd not only laid a curse on our tribe long ago when she and her ship brought illness and death, but rejected me years later when I suspected, *knew*, that it had much more to do with her father, Bjǫrn.

"Might you at least share a horn of ale with me with less of a scowl, for are we not good friends?" I implored. "And is this not a night for me to find happiness even if not in a fashion with which you approve?"

It seemed my question shook him from his brooding because we did indeed end up sharing a horn and speaking not of my desire for Freya and all she would bring to our tribe, but of village happenings in my absence.

While always good spending time with my friend, I would be lying if I said I didn't watch the gates, eagerly awaiting her arrival. Some small, worn part of me had stopped believing she might someday return and become my wife, and now it had happened. She was here and soon to be mine—if not in the flesh right away, then in little time if it were the last thing I did.

Sooner rather than later, I hoped, based on her near ethereal beauty when she finally appeared, and a hush fell over the crowd. No surprise, given the vision she presented. She wore a green dress that complemented her coloring, a ring of spring flowers on her head, and her fiery locks spilled down around her shoulders. She had once again accentuated her luminous amber eyes with coal, and she wore the white Helvig bear fur draped over her slender shoulders proudly.

Going to her, I held out my arm in offering, hardly able to catch my breath at her beauty. At the fact that I would finally become Freya Helvig's husband, as I had long dreamed. As I had wanted since I first saw her as a lad.

"You look beautiful, Freya," I said softly before speaking loud enough that all could hear. "Welcome, Freya of the Helvig clan, born of the bear." Though I need not say it, I would give her all her proper titles. "Fierce shield-maiden and seer of the north born of a strong berserker bloodline."

"Many thanks, Soren of the Dahl clan, born of the wolf," she replied dutifully, managing a small, grateful smile that she turned my people's way. Slipping her arm into mine when I knew she would prefer greeting them with her own shield and blade, she still had an impressive sword for the matrimony sheathed at her side. I assumed it had been sent along in her trunks.

Once we arrived beneath the arch, with Sten stalking alongside us, I broke tradition and presented her with the shield before we exchanged swords and rings.

"This was my mother's, and I want you to have it, just as I know she would have, before we exchange vows." I held it out to her. "You are a shield-maiden, so you should possess a shield when you become my wife."

There was no missing the flash of emotion in her eyes when she took the well-made piece carved with a fierce wolf baring its fangs.

"Thank you, Soren," she said softly, admiring it. "'Tis a fine piece. I shall wield it well."

After that, we resumed tradition as Freya presented her family sword to me with a ring on its tip.

"This is a gift from the Helvig tribe, a blade forged in our steel and wielded by my father, Bjǫrn Helvig, 'The Ferocious', born of the bear spirit and Ruler of the Berserkers, as well as a ring with the Helvig bear insignia," she said loudly enough for all to hear, handing them to me. "May you wield and wear them proudly, Soren Dahl."

I nodded with approval, praising the quality of both pieces as I sheathed the sword, slipped on the ring, and presented my sword and ring in turn after they were handed to me.

"This is a gift from the Dahl tribe, a blade forged in our steel, given to you by my mother, Aslaug Dahl, who never wielded it but had it made for you, Freya Helvig, so that you might wield it proudly when you returned to these shores and to me," I said, to many murmurs of awe from my people and a look of surprise from Freya. "As well as a ring I had forged for you; may you wear the wolf as proudly as you do the bear, Freya."

"'Tis incredible," she praised, after gazing at it with pleasure. She slipped it on, then took the sword, impressed with its weight and the intricate design on its hilt, portraying the bear and wolf standing strong alongside each other. I could tell by her expression she had questions about it and my mother, but she set them aside for now and sheathed the blade so the ceremony could proceed.

Next, our wrists were bound together with a cord, handfasting us with a tied knot, while we exchanged our vows and finally belonged to each other as it always should have been. All the while, I was acutely aware of Freya's warm wrist against mine, wishing it were her entire body wrapped up in my arms.

Although I couldn't have that quite yet because I had made her a promise, she'd made me one too, and I fully intended to take advantage of it. So, after we exchanged vows and our wrists were unbound, I did not let her get away so easily. Rather, I finally did what I had wanted to do years ago when I reeled her into my arms, cupped her soft cheek, and closed my lips over hers.

While not a long kiss because people were already roaring with approval and ready for more celebrations, it wasn't as short as she might have hoped, either. Then again, given the way she tensed initially and then softened against me, I sensed she might not have been opposed to continuing. Yet if we did, and I deepened the exchange, wrapping my tongue with hers, we might never continue with the evening's festivities.

That in mind, however difficult, I ended the kiss slowly,

pleased to find her eyes dewy with desire when they met mine. Which, in truth, made it particularly hard to pull away when all I wanted to do was scoop her up into my arms, carry her back to our lodge, and spend the next several fortnights loving her.

Instead, we made our way to the great lodge where a feast awaited, but first came Freya and me, sharing an ale and toasting the gods.

"Here is to Odin, our All Father, and Thor," I said loudly enough for all to hear, holding up my ale. "*Skald!*"

"And to Freya, the Goddess of Love." Freya held up her ale as well. "May she bless this union. *Skald!*"

"*Skald!*" Everyone roared and drank as we sat beside each other at the head table, and food was served. After Ivar sat beside me and Brynhild beside Freya, we enjoyed a fine feast of freshly caught game, seasoned salmon, flavorful cabbage stew, as well as a variety of other vegetables, bread, and churned butter.

And of course, plenty of ale.

"'Tis truly stunning," Freya said at one point, admiring the ring I had made for her to match the wolf on the hilt of her new blade. Her gaze rose to me. "Did you have it forged at the same time as the sword? And did your mother truly have the foresight to have such an impressive blade made for today's ceremony?" Her voice softened. "I now know how she cared for me when I was ill, and I'm truly grateful." She shook her head. "I had no idea because the memories were lost with my sickness. Nor did my parents ever tell me."

When I glanced at my aunt, she merely lowered her eyes, telling me she hadn't had a chance to share everything with Freya, and in all honesty, that was all right because I would prefer to share when we were alone.

"We will speak more when we retire for the evening, my new wife," I replied, liking the feel of that on my tongue very much. "Yet I can tell you now that *ja*, my mother was gifted in the ways of seers just as you are. Though yours is a warrior's soul and hers was as a healer, you are kindred."

"Then she saw me wedding you." She searched my eyes. "And you knew…you always knew."

"I always hoped," I clarified. "Whilst talented, Mother was not as strong in the ways of the gods as 'tis told you and your sisters are, but *ja*, she had great hope." I rested my hand over hers on the table, never meaning anything so much. "As did I from the moment I first saw you."

"'Twas a long time ago," she murmured, *reminded*. "And we but children."

"Even so." Wrapping my fingers with hers, I gazed into her luminous eyes. "I took one look, and I knew." I shook my head. "'Twas not your sisters I wanted by my side, but you, Freya. Always you. And 'twill never change."

"Your family, *you*, asked for my hand in marriage years ago, did you not?" she wondered softly, her gaze lingering on our joined hands before her lovely, if not soulful, amber gaze returned to my face. "And my father rejected it?"

"We, *I*, did," I admitted. "And *ja*, I was not suitable enough for you yet, so I made sure I someday would be."

"Yet you took a wife in the meantime."

"I did, at my father's request as 'twas told your father intended to promise you to another before he was injured," I revealed, wondering if she knew. "So, I did as my father asked for the sake of our tribe."

"I didn't know my father denied you," she said, confirming what I had suspected, her gaze never leaving my face. "'Twas difficult for you, then?" She tilted her head in question. "Yet mayhap you found a good union with your wife, regardless? Mayhap even love?"

"'Twas…" How to phrase it delicately? Respectfully? "An admirable companionship. We were very different from each other, and our marriage, whilst advantageous to our parents, was not what she would have wished if she'd been able to choose her own husband."

"I'm sorry to hear that." She considered what I had shared

before she gave me more than I anticipated. "I would think you, a Dahl, and the son of the earl at the time, would have made her a good match indeed."

"No doubt I did." I thought back on those days and the truths that had always lain between me and my late wife, whether we spoke of them or not. "But our hearts always lay elsewhere, and that, no matter how hard we tried, would always divide us."

I could tell by the flash of surprise and perhaps sadness in her eyes that there was no need to elaborate. My wife had loved another before we married, just as I'd loved Freya. We had tried to move past it and find love together, but our hearts were already tied to someone else, and we were never able to move much beyond a mild friendship. Yet I mourned her death because it came too soon. She dined with the gods now, though, offering those who had cared for her comfort.

We had little time to talk after that as my bard sang tales of the Dahls and our incredible feats to impress Freya and to remind our people that our ancestors were always with us, even as they were with our All Father. He sang of my accomplishments and Freya's shield-maiden prowess, painting an impressive picture of those who now led them.

As the evening wore on, we even danced and laughed, our friendship picking up where it had left off years before, then we bid everyone farewell for the night, eager to spend time alone and talk. Or so we tried until someone called out, wondering which six witnesses would follow us to our bedchamber to ensure we consummated our marriage.

This was where things would become tricky, and I could only hope, for Freya's sake, that my idea to see through her request worked. Otherwise, she would have no choice but to spread her lovely thighs for me this very eve.

CHAPTER SEVEN
Freya

WHERE I HAD thought I would feel nothing but trepidation when I met Soren on the shores of his village to marry, I instead felt a strange sense of relief and even elation when I laid eyes on him once more. It almost felt like coming home despite the distance between me and my people.

He was as handsome as ever in his black fur cloak, only now he had woven small braids into his hair with dark blue beads, the same color of the stone around my neck.

Every moment after that seemed etched in my mind and heart in a way I hadn't anticipated, as he gifted me with his mother's shield, we exchanged blades and rings, and I learned how much his late mother had foreseen. As I felt her once more stirring in my memory, like I had when speaking with Brynhild earlier.

Yet nothing stirred me more than when Soren pulled me into his arms and kissed me after we were married. I hadn't expected it and had no idea how to fight it until I felt the warmth of his lips against mine, and realized there was no fight to be had but something else. Something more profound than the heat he invoked in me when warmth turned into a searing blaze and I returned his kiss. If that were not enough, I wanted more and nearly groaned with need had he not ended the exchange first.

After that, the evening was truly enjoyable, despite the sad revelation that my father had, in fact, rejected my marriage to Soren years ago. Brynhild spent ample time with me, smiling and friendly, when Soren was otherwise preoccupied, but his second-in-command and friend, Ivar, mostly scowled if not outright ignored me. Though I didn't understand his dislike of me, I refused to let it ruin my night getting to know my new tribe.

Eventually, however, after much unexpected laughter and even dancing, Soren declared it was time for us to retire. Yet, it seemed things might not go as I had hoped when his people wondered at the witnesses who would oversee our consumma-tion. Having forgotten that some tribes still honored this age-old tradition, I tensed, wondering if Soren would be able to keep his promise to me after all.

"My people," he called out, pulling me against his side and wrapping his fingers with mine in a way I had come to like in little time. His gaze swept over everyone as the room quieted, eager for his next word, reflecting the respect and command he had over his people. "'Tis the bear and the wolf coming together and that, as my mother and our beloved queen in her own right, Aslaug Dahl, once said, is sacred and blessed and should be for their eyes alone lest the gods be offended."

Before anyone could respond, he lowered his head in prayer, prompting all to follow, and squeezed my hand ever-so-slightly. "So now I asked the gods, before all of you, if 'tis still her wish, might they send us a sign from Valhalla."

I bit back a smile that he recalled the trick I once played on him. Going along with it, I gasped loudly and unsheathed Aslaug's blade at my side, acting astonished. "'Tis warming as if being forged once more."

"Surely not," Soren exclaimed, looking at me and the blade with shock.

When we were children, I once convinced him my dagger had been touched by the gods because the metal was hot to the touch, so surely I'd been blessed and he must do my bidding, which was great fun. In truth, I had left it lying in the sun unsheathed for too long. Naturally, he figured it out eventually and played a trick or two on me in return.

Having captured the crowd's attention, I held out my new blade to Soren, sure he would play along. "Feel for yourself, husband. 'Tis warming as if your mother and I dare say the gods agree with you."

Quite serious, he murmured another prayer to the gods and his late mother and tentatively touched the metal, only to act as if it burned him. Pulling his hand back sharply, he exclaimed that it was indeed hot, as if newly forged. Surely this meant we should heed his mother's wishes.

When Ivar muttered something under his breath and narrowed his eyes at me, I feared he would reveal our ruse, but Brynhild acted first, as if she knew Ivar would cause issues. She touched the blade then yanked her hand back as if burned, her gaze wide with disbelief, before she lowered her head in prayer.

It became clear, as everyone followed her lead, that Brynhild had nearly as much sway over the crowd as Soren, because all truly believed it, and we were wished a happy consummation. May the gods watch over us always.

Wasting no time, Soren thanked his people and pulled me after him, grinning and winking once we were free of the lodge and prying eyes. Better still, free of six witnesses determined to watch me lose my virginity. Grateful for his quick thinking, I couldn't help but chuckle as he put a finger to his lips, urging me to remain quiet lest anyone overhear us, and led me down a familiar path past my cottage to the impressive lodge beside it.

"But of course 'tis yours," I said when he led me inside and shut the door behind us. The lodge had been prepared for a matrimonial evening, from the warm, inviting fire to multiple jugs of ale and mead, as well as choice meats and sweets.

My gaze drifted to the sizeable bed laden with plush furs, and I tried not to imagine the possibilities. Though I had enjoyed the evening and his kiss, I still wasn't ready for that and what it entailed, and I said so.

"Would I have gone to all that effort to do away with witnesses if I intended to ravish you?" Soren chastised lightly, a smile in his smoky blue gaze. He urged me to sit so that we might enjoy a drink and conversation alone as man and wife, and may other things happen when the time was right.

"Nay, 'tis hard to imagine you would yet still," I said carefully, accepting the ale he poured for me and speaking bluntly because I felt comfortable enough. "You now have the authority to go back on your word even in private. Even without prying eyes."

"Yet mayhap you forget I follow the old ways, not the new religion." Drink in hand, he stoked the flames on the hearth and sat beside me in front of the fire. When he looked at me once more, he grew serious.

Admittedly, my heart soared at his words. I knew he meant them, yet still. It seemed too good to be true. *He* seemed too good. And I had long learned to be wary of that.

"And what of me?" I tested him, sipping my ale. "What if I ever treat you poorly or lie with another?"

"The same would apply," he said easily enough without any warning in his tone. Just truth. "I would divorce you and send you back to your tribe without anything you gained through our marriage." There was no missing the pain in his voice after he paused, contemplating how best to phrase his wishes. "Yet 'tis my fondest hope we share something more genuine than I had with my last wife. That there is enough love, honesty, and respect betwixt us that we would never do such things to one another."

Though his love for me had been hinted at enough since we came together again, I was glad he didn't profess it for me now. That told me he wished to rediscover each other and build it together going forward.

"You're not what I expected, Soren," I said softly, giving him the truth now that I could admit our childhood friendship impacted us more than I realized. "Yet everything I think a part of me hoped you might someday be."

"'Tis good to hear." He offered me the sort of soft smile I could get used to. "So now that we're alone and starting anew in the best way possible, what would you know of me, Freya?"

Feeling my stone warm against my chest, I looked from his mother's shield and sword back to him, then finally pulled the pendant Tove had given me out of my pocket and handed it to him. "I would have you explain why my sister gave me this before I left. How I have a pendant that was clearly made by you or your mother for the wolf is the very same?"

Pain flickered in his eyes at the sight of it, and a low, barely audible sigh escaped his lips. He stared at it for a long, heartfelt moment before replying.

"'Twas made by my mother." Gazing at it fondly, he brushed his finger over it as if cherishing being able to touch it again. His attention returned to me. "Given to you on your deathbed when you were a child."

My heart leapt into my throat, and a strange chill raced through me. "What do you mean by my 'deathbed'?"

As if grappling with a difficult memory, he squeezed his hand around it, pain flashing in his eyes again. "I mean, you were so sick that even though my mother did her best to save you, you died, Freya."

I shook my head, confused, so he went on.

"I was there, hidden in the shadows of my mother's cottage, more often than she would have liked while she tried to bring you back to good health," he revealed, his voice hoarse with emotion. "I watched you turn blue and heard the death rattle as you took your final breath, then watched my mother weep over you…" As if he were back there and in denial of what he witnessed, he shook his head. "So I did all I could. Knowing it was far stronger than anyone realized, I brought the power of the wolf to you."

"I don't understand," I whispered, yet the talisman warming

at my chest told me I did. That I always had understood in some strange way.

His gaze dropped to the pendant in his palm. "My parents had this made for me at birth, and it kept me strong. Gave me hope that someday our tribe would be stronger than all the rest. That *I* would see it strong if my father could not." His eyes rose to me again. "That day, when you died, I ran to you and pressed it into your palm, willing it to give you the same strength it had given me, desperate for it to save you."

Gazing at him, I struggled to breathe. All I could manage were whispered words. "And did it?"

"*Ja.*" He wrapped his hand around the pendant again as if cherishing it. "Moments later, you gasped your first breath in minutes and your eyes fluttered open to mine." He shook his head in disbelief. "'Twas as if the gods brought you back. As though you had been searching for me wherever you went and came back when you felt this pendant. When you heard my pleas. Mayhap even my heart."

"Or mayhap your soul," I murmured, unsure why I said it, only that it felt right, yet again like the whisper of a dream or memory. As if an echo across the great halls of our gods, calling me back to Midgard...calling me home. I didn't realize I spoke my thoughts aloud until I finished it with, "And I thank you for that, Soren."

"You need never thank me," he said softly, his gaze still on my face, his heart in his eyes. "'Twas not your time and the gods agreed."

"And what of your mother?" I asked, my voice hoarse with emotion. "What happened after that? I know nothing of her death other than it came too early, *ja*? Too early when hers was only ever a caring, healing soul."

I could tell by the sadness and concern that flashed in his eyes that he would rather not say.

"Please," I insisted gently. "What happened to her?"

Though he hesitated a moment longer, he finally relented.

"My mother passed shortly thereafter from the same illness that nearly took you, but not before she insisted your blade be forged."

My vision blurred with tears at what he implied. "Surely 'twas not because of me…because she cared for me?" I swallowed hard, long convinced that certain illnesses could be spread by close proximity to the ill. "Surely she didn't catch it from me."

Yet even as I said it, I knew she had.

"She knew the risks in caring for you, Freya," he said, trying to comfort me. "Yet she insisted because she thought you were special, and she was right. More than that, she felt we were destined to be together, uniting two of Norway's most powerful tribes, and strengthening our kingdom." He took my hand again and shook his head. "She wouldn't want you to feel guilty or mourn her passing. 'Twas her choice to care for you because she was the best at what she did. Rather, she would prefer you care for her people now that you have returned."

"And care for you," I said softly, sad yet honored by his mother's kind heart and courage in tending to me when she knew it could risk her own life. "Just as you cared for me that day so long ago."

"*Ja*, I believe that would make her happy," he confessed, looking at me quite seriously again. "Yet she would not want you caring for me to repay a debt but because you feel as genuinely for me as I do for you."

I felt caught in his steady gaze, unable to look away, suspecting I was already well on my way to caring for him. Instead of saying what was in my heart, I merely nodded and said what would keep me out of his bed for now. "As I'm sure you understand, 'twill take time."

"Of course," he said easily enough. A soft, knowing smile hovered on his lips as if he knew full well I wasn't saying what I felt. He squeezed my hand gently in reassurance before going to a trunk in the corner, pulling something out, and returning.

Threading a thin leather cord through my wolf pendant, he

crouched in front of me and looked at me in a way that habitually made my breath catch. "Might I put this on you, wife, as 'twas always meant to be with you? Always to protect you."

"*Ja,*" I managed, lifting my hair and leaning forward enough that I could see the little flecks of silvery-gray in his deep-set eyes. See how close his lips were to mine as he tied the cord. Rather than pull away, his fingers lingered on the pendant, and his gaze rose to my face in a moment that seemed to somehow transcend time. As if all the years that had separated us fell away and we'd circled back to where we were always meant to be.

"I look forward to many years of gazing into your eyes like this, Freya." He dusted his weapon-roughened fingers along my jawline until he swiped the pad of his thumb across my lower lip as if eager to taste it again. "Of touching you…of knowing you are by my side."

Where I thought he might lean in and kiss me, his attention returned to my neck as if drawn there, and he readjusted the cord holding my talisman so that it rested just above the pendant.

"'Tis as if they belong together," he murmured. "As though…" His gaze narrowed. "Mayhap really, truly meant to be together."

Intrigued, I craned my neck down to peer at them where they hung just above my breasts, realizing what he meant, surprised I hadn't seen the possible connection sooner.

"It cannot be." After removing the stone from my neck, I angled it just right and slid it into a pocket above the wolf's eyes, shocked when it clicked into place. Remarkably, it was situated in a spot I'd always felt helped me see things others could not. A location of great divination. Even more interesting? The stone, combined with the metal, made it appear the same stormy blue gray as Soren's.

"'Tis of the gods," Soren exclaimed in awe.

"And of a wolf," I said softly, reminding him that the gray wolf had delivered the stone to me as a child. Then, the origins of the pendant. "Not to mention a fellow seer." My gaze rose to his face. "Yet 'twas you who knew to give it to me. You who brought me back from the land of the dead."

When his gaze met mine once more, what passed between us was impossible to describe. Almost as if Thor invoked a bolt of lightning one could feel but not see. A tangible jolt that made our pupils flare and energy fluctuate between us.

Where I thought once again he would close the distance and kiss me, he instead closed his eyes for a moment before he opened them to me, shook his head, and returned to his chair.

"'Twill not be easy, if not the greatest challenge of my life, but I'm determined to honor your wishes not to lie together until you're ready." He refreshed our ales. "So let us talk more of everything we missed of one another's lives and get to know each other again, *ja?*"

Understanding how close he had come to kissing me and wanting far more, I was grateful for his inner strength to step away. Or so I kept telling myself.

"I would like that." Doing my best to temper my own desire, I sipped my ale. "Where should we begin?"

Little did I expect where he thought that should be, but then it soon became clear there might be even more to what hung around my neck now.

Better still, what it meant for the wolf and the bear to come together.

CHAPTER EIGHT

Soren

IT WAS HARD to explain how I felt when Freya's runic stone, then the pendant I had given her years ago drew my eyes, other than it was an otherworldly pull.

A sense of certainty I had never felt before.

And it turned out to be right when the stone clicked into place inside the pendant as if the two had been made for one another, just like I had long felt Freya and I were.

If that were not telling enough, the sensation that passed between us when the stone found its rightful place in the pendant certainly was. It felt like some kind of strange, unexplainable yet powerful, mystical energy.

At that moment, I had never wanted to bring her to my bed more. Wanted to ravish her until she cried out in pleasure. Yet I was a man of my word, so I forced myself to return to my chair and continued talking rather than doing what I really wanted to do. Rather than doing what I knew would bridge the gap between us faster than anything else, because I suspected it would be intense.

While I meant to speak of lighter things, the words that passed my lips seemed made of all the magic brewing between us, because what else could I call it? Love? Yes. But magic, too. Great power born of the gods and a destiny that was ours. A path we must follow.

So, I asked what I felt needed asking the most.

"Why do you not use your seer abilities anymore, Freya?" I said. "Why do you not divine for others?"

Although clear, given the flattening of her lips and the way she took several gulps of ale, she had not expected the question, Freya was wise enough to realize I deserved to know, as our people would want to understand, too.

"I do use them still, or should I say they use me to stay connected to my sisters when I'm not with them," she confessed. "I imagine 'tis because of the stones." Hesitating, she struggled to share before continuing. "My sisters aside, I don't use my gift anymore because the last time I did, it did not warn my mother of impending danger but instead seemed to lead her to slaughter."

I gently prompted her to continue when her haunted gaze lingered on the flames, as if she stared back in time at something only she could see. "How so?"

"I foresaw safe passage for her through the wilds of our homeland before our family moved to the isle." Struggling with her emotions, she clenched her jaw for a moment before continuing. "As you know, our Norwegian tribes tend to battle each other more than they should, and whilst she was a good fighter, she was not..." She blinked back tears and took another swig of ale. "She was not enough, and she and her companions were slain before they could make it to a nearby village."

"I'm so sorry, Freya," I said softly, wrapping my fingers with hers where they rested on the table. Although there was nothing I could say to ease her grief, I had to try. "My mother once told me that divination can mean many things, yet everything mystics such as yourself foresee is divine. 'Tis the path the gods want us to walk so things go as they should. She claimed Odin himself would someday reward seers for aiding in a tapestry of life much richer and more pre-destined than any of us will ever realize. So even if it seems you steered your mother wrong, 'twas always the path she was meant to walk."

"Whilst wise words, you can understand how they might ring hollow for a daughter who feels responsible for her mother's death," she murmured, her gaze still on the flames. "Father was never the same after that. Then weeks later, he was attacked by the bear, which I didn't warn him of because I had shunned my gift. So you see how I could be blamed not just for my mother's death but my father's downfall. After that, he refused to allow me and my sisters to fight again and risk losing everything he cared about." She shook her head and vowed, "And for that I will forever steer clear of divination lest it skew everything I love once more."

Even though she should not be faulted for either, I understood, at least for the moment, she wasn't ready to forgive herself. Hopefully, in time, I would be able to help her move past the weight she was determined to carry on her shoulders. For now, however, I steered the conversation away from such sadness, intending to revisit it later, when her emotions were less raw.

Unfortunately, I sensed her sadness and frustration had gotten the better of her on a night I would have wished otherwise, and she pleaded exhaustion shortly thereafter.

"I should return to my cottage," she began, but trailed off when I shook my head.

"Nay, 'tis not something you can do anytime soon, Freya," I reminded. "We were fortunate enough that we didn't need witnesses to our consummation. To that end, 'tis crucial you sleep in this lodge for the foreseeable future. The cottage was only ever a place meant for you to go if you wanted time alone, but not at night when you should be in your husband's bed."

Her gaze swept over the room, lingering on my bed before she looked at the doorway leading to adjoining rooms. "Are there more beds here or just the one?"

"Just the one," I said. "The other rooms will be for our children, and beds to come once they are with us. If you would like,

I'll retire to one of those rooms whilst you change into your sleeping gown if you desire to wear one, but we will rest in the same bed." I shook my head. "And I will not touch you lest you want to be touched."

"'Tis a lot to ask of you," she said, relief in her eyes. "But, *ja*, I would appreciate a moment to change in privacy."

While tempted to ask her why she feared intimacy, because I sensed she did, I refrained for now and made my way out the back rather than linger in one of the rooms. Drawing in the cool air, I tried not to envision her changing so close to me, longing for the moment I would at last feel the weight of her in my bed, even if I could not touch her tonight. Rather, I focused on the sound of the trees brushing against each other in the wind. The sight of the clouds rushing past a nearly full moon.

By the time I made my way back in, she was beneath my furs, seemingly sound asleep, and nothing touched my heart more. It had seemed like an impossible dream that she might ever truly be mine, yet there she was, in my bed. I sat again, enjoyed one last ale, and admired her, sensing she was not truly sleeping. It turned out I was right because her breathing soon slowed, telling me she had finally drifted off.

After finishing my ale, I undressed and crawled into bed beside her, wishing I could pull her against me, but I knew better. If I did, I might never let go. Moreover, I would want to close my lips over hers again and explore every last part of her. Love her in ways I had long imagined. Fortunately, an incredible sense of comfort, if not peace, settled over me at her mere proximity, and I dozed off faster than I thought possible.

When I stirred awake at daybreak, she still slept soundly, only now she faced in my direction and wore a soft smile as if she, too, had found contentment being so close to me. A contentment that kept her from rising early like she usually did in our youth. Helpless to do anything but admire her delicate beauty for a time, I finally forced myself to rise, dress, add wood to the dying embers, and leave, when all I wanted to do was settle between her thighs.

When Sten, standing protectively outside our door, looked at me as if I shouldn't be awake so early, given the beautiful woman in my bed, I shrugged and nodded in agreement. "What can I tell you other than that I'm a man of my word?"

Somehow, I wasn't surprised when he remained guarding our door instead of joining me as I made my way past smiths hammering glowing iron at open-air forges and fisherman preparing their boats, down to the end of a pier to watch the sun rise. My wolf had taken to Freya straight off, just as I had. Breathing in the chilly, salt-ridden air, I took in the deep melons splashed across the sky, and imagined many mornings like this with her by my side.

"How did I know you would be here alone at an hour you should still be wrapped in your wife's arms?" came Ivar's gruff voice when he joined me. Crossing his arms over his chest, he gazed at the sea and shook his head. "She has shunned you already, has she not?" He eyed me knowingly. "How else to explain that farce you two put on last night because 'twas a farce indeed."

Ivar might be a brute to most, but few were more observant or wise.

"Might it not have been a desire to consummate our vows in private?" I countered. "And might she not be sound asleep at this very moment, well satisfied after a night in each other's arms?"

"She might, but I doubt it, given the rumors about her," Ivar grunted. "Rumors most in these parts don't know. They hear only the tales of her battle prowess and seer abilities." He gave me a pointed look. "Yet we both know she is considered cold to men. That she would not take a husband even if she had free rein to do so."

Somehow, I wasn't surprised Ivar knew, as he was used to looking after my welfare when it came to Freya and my never-ending desire for her. Nevertheless, it was no longer his place to say such things, and I made that clear.

"What my wife and I do together is no one's concern but ours." I returned his pointed look. "And you would do well to remember that, my friend."

Ivar considered me for a long moment, then sighed and grunted something indiscernible under his breath before sharing news. "Rumors are coming out of the south that there is unrest in Scotland," he said. "Rumors that we're losing ground there and King Hákon might soon be calling on several of his stronger clans to do his bidding."

I frowned. "And what would that be?"

"'Tis unclear as of yet, but I suspect he won't want to give up the last of Norway's stake there." He shook his head and eyed the south gravely. "Even though I suspect 'tis a battle and land already lost, mark my words, there will be fighting first, and lives will once more be lost."

"'Tis hard to imagine it might all be gone soon," I said, sensing more change on the horizon. "From the great Danelaw centuries ago to barely a foothold there now, despite all we have given that country."

"*Ja*," Ivar agreed. "Yet times are changing, and we look to other lands. The Baltics. New paths. New places. A stronger Norway."

"Indeed," I murmured, even as we both knew, despite a great love for our king, that things would need to change here first, to quell the last of civil unrest and warring tribes.

Although Ivar and I spoke briefly about other things while seeing to a few boats, my thoughts remained on Freya. I might enjoy battling, but I hoped this time the king would not call on me, giving me no choice but to leave her so soon. I wanted time for us to grow closer. Make her fall in love with me. Yet my mind kept going back to the crack that had formed on her boat. I could only pray it was not an omen meant to separate us once more.

Almost as if she sensed my troubled thoughts, Freya appeared on the shoreline with Sten beside her, and all I could do was stare for a moment, taken by the sight of her in her white fur cloak with her hair braided back. When her gaze met mine, I felt the same intense connection I had experienced the night before, despite the distance between us.

Joining her and Sten, I couldn't help but smile. "It seems Sten had taken to you, Freya."

"So it seems." She looked at the wolf not cautiously, as most would, but fondly. "He's quite impressive." Her gaze returned to me. "How did he end up with you? 'Tis a rare thing to achieve such devotion from a wolf."

"'Tis." I urged her to join me so that we might eat together. "'Twas a stroke of good luck for him to be sure, and mayhap me as well. I was out hunting one snowy night and came across him and his litter mates when they were pups." Recalling the gruesome scene, I shook my head. "A sizeable bear was attacking them, and whilst I managed to injure it, I was unable to slay it. Either way, I ended up driving it off, but not before it killed all of Sten's litter mates but him, yet he barely lived."

"How awful." She frowned. "And what of his mother?"

"I found her nearby, slain as well," I replied gravely. "So I brought Sten back to my stronghold, saw to his wounds, and he survived. He was free to go after that, but never did. Not really. Occasionally, he leaves for a few days, likely to hunt or mate, but he always returns."

"You saved him, so he repays the debt." Glancing from Sten to me, she offered the sort of soft smile I could get used to seeing at the beginning of each new day. "'Tis an admirable start to your friendship that has undoubtedly become an unbreakable bond."

"And now you share that bond with him as well," I said, pleased. "'Tis telling on several fronts."

"Because the spirit of my tribe is of the very beast that took his kin," she said softly, seeing it just as clearly. "So 'tis forgiveness and acceptance of me as your mate."

"'Twould seem that way." I nodded hello to many in passing as most woke early to begin their day. "After we have our morning meal, we'll spend time amongst the people if you would like."

"I would." She nodded hello to many as well, at ease with my people, and I could not be happier. It was a promising start to our marriage, and it lent me comfort if I had to leave anytime soon.

Once I'd led her back into the lodge where we had celebrated the previous evening, we spent time chatting with people who were clearly in awe of her before joining my aunt at the head table.

"And how are you two this fine morn?" Brynhild said.

Even though she gave us a soft, knowing smile that seemed to speak to us consummating our marriage, given her actions the night before, I would suspect she knew better. Yet things must continue to seem a certain way.

"We're very well, thank you, Brynhild," Freya answered, a becoming pink in her cheeks when she glanced at me. A blush she could not fake for the sake of spinning a tale, making me wonder if she'd imagined what it would be like to see through our consummation, too, or if I merely wished that might be the case.

"'Tis good to lay eyes on that once more," Brynhild said softly, her gaze lingering on the pendant around Freya's neck after she sat across from us. "It no doubt makes my sister happy to see it where it belongs from her seat in Valhalla." She narrowed in on the blue stone inside. "And with an addition, no less."

"Did you know of this, then, Brynhild?" Freya wondered while enjoying a light fare of bread, jam, cheese, and honeyed mead. She fingered the pendant. "Were you there when your sister had this made?"

"I was," she acknowledged, surprising me. "She said 'twould someday become whole if the Wyrd unfolded as it should. She saw great destinies and a stronger Norway attached to it." Her gaze went from me to Freya. "And an equally great love."

"I don't doubt she's right," I said, hoping Freya saw in my eyes the great love I already felt for her when I looked at her. Love and admiration that would only ever grow stronger.

After that, we spoke of other things, yet all the while I remained aware of Freya by my side. The sound of her breathing and the faint, sweet scent of her hair. Every so often, I would lean closer to share one thing or another just so our shoulders touched. Other times, I brushed aside an escaped lock of fiery hair from her cheek so that I could hear the faint hitch of her breath or feel the softness of her cheek or neck.

Once we'd finished eating, Brynhild wished us well and went about her business, but not before giving me a small nod of encouragement, assuring me that I need not worry about showing Freya her boat. Yet even as I leaned close once more and told her I had one more thing I would like to give her for our wedding, I feared that crack and what it might represent.

"We will spend time among your new people after I show you," I assured her. "But first this, as 'tis something that will be all yours always. Something I hope makes you realize how much this tribe appreciates you and gives you a sense of freedom whenever you desire it, as you will always be free when with me, wife. Always Freya Helvig before Freya Dahl."

I could tell she appreciated that, and as it turned out, when I led her back to the shore, she appreciated my gift even more.

Or so was the case at first.

CHAPTER NINE

Freya

ALTHOUGH I WAS nervous the night before that Soren might break his word and lie with me after all, he did not. Instead, he didn't come to bed straight away but drank another ale, and while I tried to remain awake and on guard despite pretending to sleep, I dozed off anyway, only to stir awake hours later.

At first, I remained perfectly still, getting my bearings, only to discover Soren sleeping soundly beside me. The furs covered him from the waist down, leaving the rest of his nude form exposed, and it was as impressive as I had suspected it would be. I could still hardly believe the scrawny boy from my youth had become so well-formed, yet he had. From his broad shoulders and muscular arms to the hard ridges of his torso, he was well worth admiring. I took in the various tattoos inked into his skin, recognizing many runic symbols within them, glad he still practiced the old ways.

Where I thought I wouldn't be able to fall back asleep, given he was so close without clothing, I felt surprisingly at ease and must have drifted off again, because when I stirred awake, he was gone, and the sun had crested the horizon. It was hard to recall the last time I didn't wake before the sun, yet here I was in Soren's bed doing so. If that were not enough, I felt a nugget of disappointment that he wasn't still here when I thought I would feel relief.

Rather, that feeling came once I dressed and locked eyes with him at the shore. And it only intensified when he smiled and closed the distance. Now, having enjoyed our morning meal together, he claimed he had something else he wanted to gift me with before visiting with his people, and led me back to the shore.

"This way." He took my hand and brought me down one of the piers, stopping in front of an impressive, well-made boat with a bear and wolf carved side by side into the bow. "I had this built for you, my new wife. 'Tis your own boat, so that you might sail when you wish, whether with me or not."

Stunned, it took me a moment to find my voice. "Truly?" I looked from him back to the boat. "'Tis mine?"

"'Tis." He climbed down into it, urging me to follow, and looked at me with an expectant smile. "What do you think?"

"I think you have very talented boat builders." I returned his smile and joined him. "With an equally talented aunt overseeing everything."

"She built a great deal of this one herself, or should I say everything she could handle at her age," he divulged. "'Twas important to us both that you liked it."

"And I do," I exclaimed, more than touched. Running my hands along the side, I was impressed by its smooth edges and attention to detail. "I cannot express how thankful I am, Soren." After taking in the expert craftsmanship of the hull for another moment, I looked at him, truly humbled by such a gesture. The sheer lengths he had gone to see me content in my new home. "This makes me happier than you know."

"'Tis very good to hear," he returned, his eyes a vivid bluish gray backdropped by the water.

Our eyes lingered on each other for a moment before I continued taking in the boat, especially drawn to the carving at the front because it matched the hilt of my new blade. Not just that, but I liked more by the moment, the depiction of the bear and wolf shoulder to shoulder, standing strong together, just as I sensed Soren and I would.

"Let's take her out," Soren suggested. I couldn't help but to agree. Before long, we were setting sail. Cool winds filled our sails and warm sunshine caressed our faces. The simmering sensual feelings Soren inspired were even more evident between us whenever he stepped close to show me one thing or another, or when our eyes met. I knew it was a moment I would cherish forever because here, on the waves with the scent of salt in my nostrils and the seawind in my hair, our friendship flourished once more. I found myself laughing more than I had in a very long time. I felt at home.

Pleased by how the boat moved on the waves, I made my way to the front and admired the details in the carving, only for the pendant to warm against my chest. Compelled, my gaze drifted down and locked on a small crack. Struggling to breathe, I ran my finger along it, startled when such intense heartache, worry, and fear surged through me that tears sprang to my eyes.

"'Twill not get any larger, nor will it affect the boat's performance," Soren appeared at my side to assure me, looking at me with a mix of confusion and worry. "I promise you that."

"Yet it will get larger in another way," I whispered, my voice hoarse with emotion despite how much I wished it otherwise, given it was my gift of prophecy at work. "Because it represents us and a great divide ahead. A rift. Distance growing betwixt us…" When I trailed off and looked at him because it felt like there was more to this, his troubled expression confirmed my worry. "What is it, Soren? What do you know about this crack?"

"I know a similar one formed on your parents' ship the last time you were here," he revealed, sighing. "Shortly before you crossed over to the land of the dead, taking you away from me, however briefly."

Swallowing back another sharp surge of emotions at the implication, I rested my hand on his arm, trying to lend him comfort. Both of us comfort, if I were to be honest.

"And 'tis that you must focus on," I said softly. "That 'twas not a permanent separation betwixt us, for am I not alive and returned? Am I not your wife now?"

"You are," he said just as softly, resting his hand over mine and gazing into my eyes. "And if ever you try to go to the land of the dead again before your time, I will do everything in my power to pull you back once more."

Captured by his steady blue-gray gaze, I saw the truth of it in his eyes. He would chase me into the afterlife and mayhap even into the great halls of Valhalla if I traveled there too soon, despite it being a warrior's honor.

"Let us hope, then, it doesn't come to that," I managed, pulling away when his gaze dropped to my lips, and I sensed he longed to kiss me.

While I could admit I liked it a great deal the first time, I strongly suspected it would lead to more, and I still needed time. More of a chance to push past this terrible anxiety and trepidation my attacker had left me with, despite knowing Soren would not hurt me. He had proven it last night when he left me untouched.

"Again, thank you for this impressive boat," I said dutifully. "I've never been so honored." Tilting my head in question, I issued him a hopeful smile. "Might we visit with your people now?"

"I would like that," he said readily enough. "I'm sure they would like that a great deal, too."

Grateful that he didn't seem put off by my pulling away and avoiding intimacy, we continued enjoying a pleasant day together. Sometimes he was with me, and other times, away to attend to one thing or another, but he always returned with a warm smile. Moreover, despite enjoying having more time with people today than last night, I found myself looking forward to him returning to my side.

That sensation only grew over the next few weeks as I settled into my new home and role as the earl's wife, getting to know my new tribe on a more personal level while they went about their daily tasks. Although Brynhild and I grew closer, Ivar remained distant and clipped with me.

"You just need to give him time," Brynhild counseled one blustery afternoon after Ivar scowled at me for no apparent reason and stomped along like the beast I had started calling him in my mind. "His disposition has been foul of late, and he has long been protective of Soren. Since they were young lads."

"Yet what harm have I done Soren that would make Ivar dislike me so?" I frowned as we strolled in woodland near the stronghold, checking the growth of trees for shipbuilding. "And why is his disposition fouler than it once was?"

"While he claims you were at fault for bringing illness to our tribe years ago, I suspect he knows better," she said. "Not only did many on your boats fall ill, but sickness was sweeping the countryside anyway, so 'twould have touched us eventually."

Although sad things went as they had, I was practical enough to know she was right.

"I think Ivar's disposition toward you has more to do with Soren," Brynhild went on. "You must understand, 'twas not easy for him seeing you leave after your illness, given the bond he'd thought you two forged. Then to have your hand in marriage rejected years later." She shook her head. "He didn't take it well, and 'twas Ivar who saw him through both instances."

"And does Ivar know I had no choice in both cases?"

"No doubt he does, but that makes little difference until he feels you won't find a way to break Soren's heart again." She sighed and pulled her gray fur cloak tighter around her against the wind. "And as I said, his foul mood in general doesn't help things any. He's grown more worried about our country lately and the changes that are undoubtedly coming."

A strange sense of forbidding rolled through me. Could these changes be related to the crack in my boat? Might they somehow separate me and Soren once more?

When I looked at her in question, she went on.

"There is talk of strife in Scotland," she revealed. "'Tis said they revolt against the last of our presence there, and battling lies ahead."

That alarmed me on several fronts, given that my sister, Astrid, was in Scotland, and Soren and his tribe were renowned for their battle prowess.

No fool, I did not need to ask what that might mean. "So, our king could very well call on Soren and his warriors."

"'Tis a possibility," Brynhild confirmed. "'Twill depend on several factors, I imagine."

"*Ja*," I murmured, looking to the south. "This stronghold is positioned well for a swift journey past the Hebrides and advantageous approach from the north to the western shores of Scotland."

"'Tis," Brynhild concurred, her voice gentler than it had been moments before, without doubt because I wore my troubled emotions on my face, but my soul stirred in warning at this news. If the crack in my boat was not alarming enough, Soren wasn't just renowned for his battle skills, but also for ships built to withstand any storm, making him and his tribe a good choice to call upon. Now, having seen them and knowing their overseer and builder firsthand, I agreed.

Yet some weather was sent by the gods, and some ships were meant to sink, no matter how well built. I could only pray they were not our ships and my husband was not at the helm.

"And what word of the Norse still in Scotland?" I asked. "Those like my sister sent to garner good relations and mayhap make an advantageous marriage to keep things amicable betwixt the people."

"I have heard nothing of them." She looked at me with the tenderness a mother might. "Yet if I do, I will tell you straight away, even though I'm sure Soren will before it even reaches my ears."

"Despite not telling me any of this to begin with," I murmured. "No, I'm not sure he will."

"If you ask, *ja*, he will," she said. "If you have learned anything else since arriving, 'tis surely how much he cares about you. How much he longs for you to find peace and happiness by his side."

Our conversation ended after that because Brynhild was called away, leaving me to my own thoughts, and every one of them only saw an unpredictable future on mine and Soren's horizon. A fate that was indeed full of change, leading to fear not just for my new husband but also for my sister in Scotland.

So I was grateful for the distraction when I came upon warriors practicing their skills in the large clearing outside the main lodge. Slick with mud from rain the night before, the ground was more challenging for fighting, much to my pleasure, even if I could only observe for now.

Assessing the men and women alike who fought in individual battles, I could admit to being impressed if not envious, and it seemed Soren saw that as he joined me.

"Would you like to practice as well, shield-maiden?" he wondered, yet again surprising me, considering my father would have forbidden it, and I said so. While tempted for a moment not to, I had come to respect Soren a great deal, and I would not have him break his word.

"My word was to accept your shield and blade and not let you travel to distant lands and battle." The corner of his mouth inched up, and he seemed to dare me. "Nothing was said about you fighting here within this tribe." He shrugged. "Besides, as a warrior in your own right who might someday need to protect your people, I would see you practice regularly."

My heart leapt with excitement at the thought of wielding a blade against someone again after all these years. "Yet, I'm not dressed properly, nor do I have my shield and blade in hand."

"Then go get them," he urged. "You know where the weapons I gifted you are, and if you look in the trunk toward the back of our lodge, you might find clothing that suits you."

When I cocked my head and offered a questioning smile, wondering if he was serious, he met my smile and gestured that I hurry along and return so that our people might see what I was capable of.

"It's been years since Father allowed me to fight," I warned. "Do you truly want to risk my breaking their belief that I'm so fierce in battle?"

"Nay," he said, growing serious, clearly confident in my abilities. "I want to remind them just how fierce you are. That your Helvig Viking ancestors are very much alive in you, so go, wife, and return swiftly."

Bolstered by his faith in me, I headed for our lodge, not for the first time, feeling a sense of well-being upon entering that I had never felt elsewhere. A sense of finally finding my own home, often hoping Soren might be here when I dropped in through the day after going our separate ways.

In the evenings, we would sit together in front of the fire, enjoy an ale or two, and share our day. Then, we would often share more than that, as we covered all the years we had missed in between. While life had grown dull after I could no longer battle, I often spoke of those short years beforehand, and he was as enraptured by my retellings as I was by his. We might be among the last of our kind in this ever-changing Norway, but we had both fought well and were part of something that made us proud.

Sometimes we laughed, and at other times grew serious, but we always went to bed in good spirits. He kept his word, never touching me unless I allowed it. And thus far, that had only been his hand in mine. One morn, I woke to find his big, strong body curled around me, his front to my back, keeping me warm, and I liked it more than I admitted. He never took it further, though, and we rose together to watch the sunrise.

"'Tis perfect," I murmured upon opening the trunk toward the back of our lodge, grinning at several pairs of trousers suited to my size. It had been too long since I wore such, and I was beyond grateful when I put them on, followed by one of a few tunics.

After braiding my hair back more securely and shouldering into my white bear fur, I grabbed my new shield and blade, yet again pleased by them, and returned to Soren's side. Standing tall, I felt more like myself than I had in a while, pleased by the murmurs of awe rippling through my new people at my appearance. It better portrayed who I was at heart and the tales they had heard of me.

Rather than sit in the chair designated for him, Soren seemed to prefer standing with his arms crossed over his chest, assessing his warriors as they battled. He often called out moves that could use improvement and those he was pleased with.

"'Tis a good method of training," I said at one point, watching the fighting just as closely. "Giving them the good with the bad to keep their confidence up."

"As do you, it seems," he said, amused when he glanced at me. "Or mayhap you don't hear yourself, wife? For you seem to mutter under your breath all the same things I see and say."

"Do I?" I asked innocently, grinning because I suspected I did without even realizing it.

"*Ja*, and so I would ask something of you."

Curious at the challenging look in his gaze, I perked an eyebrow. "And what would that be?"

As it happened, his response more than surprised me.

CHAPTER TEN

Soren

A GROWING NEED to ravish Freya aside, I had never been so impressed or attracted to her as when she returned to battle practice, dressed in trousers and a tunic, looking every inch a shield-maiden with my mother's weapons. She was even more beautiful than she'd been on our wedding night. I nearly said so, too, but didn't want to ruin the moment and take from her concentration as she assessed our warriors battling in small groups.

Every muttered word of how she liked one move and how others needed improvement was in perfect alignment with my own assessments and spoke to her superior skills. She claimed there had only been a few years of fighting before her father no longer allowed it, but it was clearly enough for her to prove she very much descended from great shield-maidens.

Moreover, she was clearly a shield-maiden herself.

The times might not call for women to fight much, but I refused to have her feel worthless or useless when this was her calling, so I thought to redirect her talents elsewhere and hoped today might prove my idea sound. So far, it seemed promising. Yet I would have her do something for me first, so I asked her a question I knew she would not anticipate but mayhap appreciate.

"Would you battle me here and now for all to see, Freya?" I looked at her in question. "Battle me so that everyone might see what you are capable of?"

"Battle you?" Her eyebrows swept up, and a slow smile curled her mouth. The same excitement I had seen when we were on the high seas flared in her luminous amber gaze. "Fight my husband and their chieftain? The renowned Soren Dahl? *Truly?*"

Her anticipation reflected my own, and I met her small smile. "If you dare, Freya Helvig, born of the bear and fierce shield-maiden of the north."

A throaty, almost sensual-sounding chuckle bubbled up from her chest. "Oh, I dare, indeed."

Pleased, I called for all to cease fighting so that I might have the circle to spar with my wife, noting Ivar standing nearby with his arms crossed over his chest and a stoic, untrusting look on his face. Outside of me and likely Freya, none fought better, so he would watch this closely.

Murmurs of awe had already been rippling through the crowd at her changed attire and the sight of weapons in her hand, so it was no surprise that all conceded right away and cleared the area. Nor was I surprised when the crowd grew as news of us battling spread. It wasn't every day that such a thing happened between a husband and wife, never mind who Freya and I were before we came together.

All grew quiet as we set aside our fur cloaks and circled each other, holding our weapons at the ready, assessing each other's every move. Freya might not have battled for years, but her form was good if not perfect, leaving no openings, so I had no choice but to go at her as I would any other and find her weaknesses.

While some might have been more lenient, given that it was the woman he loved, and his wife no less, I knew I would lose her respect if I did. So, I moved quickly, driving her back, utilizing moves that typically made my opponent falter, but not Freya. If anything, despite my speed and battle prowess, she watched my every move and kept to defensive maneuvers as if biding her time and wearing me down.

The slick mud made our dance of blades and shields especially treacherous, but she moved with ease and grace, dodging my every thrust. Where I thought her ultimate plan was to wear me down by staying on the defensive, she ended up circling away only to go on the offensive and come back at me hard. Navigating the slick ground with ease, she pushed me back with quick, clever thrusts that kept me on guard, smoothly putting me on the defensive, whether I wanted to be there or not.

If her battle prowess wasn't enough, I realized, at least for me and without doubt many male warriors, the sight of her attacking was magnificent. Whether the polar bear adorned her shoulders or not, she fought with its ferociousness, her hair and eyes ablaze with fire in the late-day sun while she methodically sliced with her blade.

So, I came at her just as hard, thrilled at the feel of battling such a worthy opponent. On top of that, there was added excitement in the way we moved together. A fierce dance of sorts. Our aggression and rhythm were exhilarating in a way I suspected would be matched when we finally lay together.

And it only got better from there, ending in the best way possible.

Tossing our shields aside, we sparred with each other so rapidly that I slipped and fell to my back, only to find her straddling me seconds later, with our blades to one another's necks at the same time. Where some men, especially ones as esteemed as I, might be put off by the equal draw, I was never so aroused or impressed.

Never prouder to call her my friend and wife.

The crowd had grown so quiet that nothing but the wind in the trees and waves crashing in the distance could be heard as the two of us breathed heavily and gazed into each other's eyes. As it had been several times since we came back together, it felt like we connected in a way no one else could understand. In a fashion that was all ours. One that had belonged to us since the beginning of creation.

"Do you yield?" we asked at the same time, grinning at our synchronized question, our gazes holding for a long moment before she stood and held out her hand to me.

"*Ja*, husband, I yield."

"As do I, wife," I conceded, taking her hand and standing to roars of approval, reveling in everyone's looks of pride and approval at Freya. She even earned a curt nod from Ivar before he left, but that was something. A beginning when it came to my obstinate second-in-command.

Meanwhile, taking advantage of the moment, I addressed my warriors, all of whom were still present and witnessed Freya's battle skills, earning their respect based on their looks of pride. She had gone up against the best warrior they knew and held her ground until the end, and I spoke to that.

"Whilst I promised Freya's father she wouldn't go to battle with us, but bear strong sons and daughters born of the bear and wolf, 'twas just seen 'twould be wasteful not to put such skills to good use," I said loudly enough for all to hear. "Therefore, I would see that she helps train our warriors going forward until the day her father changes his mind, or something happens that makes it crucial for her to fight sooner." Sheathing my blade, I gestured proudly at her. "For is she not every inch a shield-maiden and my equal in battle?"

When roars of approval and agreement rose, Freya lowered her head in thanks, then smiled at everyone. Though someone offered her an ale, she refused. Instead, she gestured at a female warrior to step forward so that they might spar, signaling that practice should resume and drinking would follow later. Grinning, I nodded in agreement and joined my aunt, who stood nearby, with just as much pride.

"I always knew your mother was truly gifted with foresight, but this day 'twas never so clear, nephew." She admired the ease with which Freya worked with her opponent, eloquent in the way she drew out the other woman's strengths and weaknesses. "Whilst I disagree with her father's wishes, I can't help but suspect your mother foresaw Freya serving our people all the better right here, building already fierce warriors into the very best in all of Norway."

Nodding in agreement, I took great pleasure in watching Freya over the next several hours. She embraced her inner warrior, the only way she could for now, but I sensed it was enough. When her eyes occasionally met mine, and I saw the excitement burning bright within them, resurrecting her in a way that had been lacking before, I knew how grateful she was. Moreover, how promising our future looked now that she knew I would never deny her the chance to battle so long as I kept my word to her father.

Not long after, the sun sank low in the sky, its brilliant crimson fading as it dipped into the sea behind black, churning clouds. Thunder rumbled in the distance, prompting the battles to come to an end, and people left to bathe and prepare for dinner. As it was every evening, except during times of celebration, many would go to the great lodge to dine and socialize, while others chose to remain in their cottages and feast with their families.

Typically, Freya and I joined everyone in the great lodge so that she could spend time with our people, and I expected no differently tonight until she surprised me on our walk back to our lodge.

"Might we dine alone tonight, Soren?"

The softness in her voice and the almost shy way she looked at me were at odds with the fierceness that had been on her face minutes before battling.

"Or do you think it better given my new role that I'm among our people tonight so that we might drink and toast to battles well fought, even if only friendly?"

No fool, I answered as any husband in his right mind would.

"I think our people would well understand if we wanted to remain in this eve, given we're still newly married," I replied, aware that Sten stalked along after us, now not just my protector but Freya's. "And I would very much like it."

Although I was unsure what it might mean or if anything sensual would come of it, I enjoyed her company, finding our friendship as strong as it ever was, so time alone was always welcome. To that end, I spoke to someone in passing about having our meal brought to us. Soon after, we entered our lodge to a freshly tended fire, a basin of steaming water, and ale and food to snack on.

Sitting in front of the fire, Freya poured us ale and grinned at me before downing half of it. When she smiled again, my heart warmed at her happiness.

"Yet again, I find myself grateful to you for all the kindness you have shown me." Freya shook her head, seeming to marvel at it. "'Twas so much more than I anticipated and it has…" She seemed to struggle with finding the right words to express what was in her heart. "It's made me so pleased that you sought me to be your wife." Her eyes lingered on mine. "That you never gave up on me."

"Nor would I ever," I vowed, meaning every word. "You make me very proud, Freya. Not just years ago or today but always."

"As do you, me," she said softly, her gaze faltering a moment before she drank down the rest of her ale in one long swig and set her mug down. "So, I want you to know more about why I've feared lying with you thus far. You have earned the truth."

Setting aside my ale without drinking it, I nodded for her to continue.

Even though she hesitated as if she might not go on, rallied her courage, and spoke. "'Twas a night much like this with a storm brewing." She swallowed hard. "Mother had already died, and Father was away. Warriors from another tribe were passing through, and whilst most were good men, it turned out one was not and cornered me behind a lodge during celebrations."

I tensed at the mix of frustration and sadness saturating her eyes.

"Though a good warrior, I was without my blade and caught unaware and…" She trailed off, clearly struggling with what had happened. "'Twas terrifying and fast, and he would have taken my virtue against that wall had my sister, Astrid, not appeared and whipped a dagger into his leg." Releasing a strained chuckle, she shook her head. "The sister who, while a warrior, would choose words over violence, saved me in ways she will never truly understand because he staggered off without accomplishing what he hoped."

Wishing I could strangle this stranger with my bare hands, I clenched my fists. "And what happened to this man?"

"He left shortly thereafter with his fellow warriors and died months later in battle," she managed, her gaze on the flames. "So, I never had my revenge, yet I walked away unscathed."

Not nearly, but I didn't point that out right now. "Did you not tell your father? Surely Bjǫrn would have sought justice."

"I was going to, but the bear attacked him whilst he was away, and when he returned the next day…" She shook her head. "'Twas no time to tell him such a thing, for his recovery was long and difficult, and his disposition much changed. Even if I had wanted to pursue my attacker with a blade in hand and cut off his ballocks, I had to stay. Had to help my father back to health and then become the daughter he insisted I be after that."

Sad for the path the Norns had led her down, I set aside my quiet rage and need for revenge on a man who was no more and did all I could for now. I crouched in front of her, wrapped my fingers with hers, and gazed into her eyes with all the tenderness I felt for her. "I cannot tell you how sorry I am for what you suffered, Freya. Even though you kept your virtue, 'twas undoubtedly terrifying and you deserved your revenge," I said solemnly, understanding her warrior's soul enough to know how crucial that was. How helpless that man had made her feel when she was the most capable woman I had ever met. "What I can vow, however, is that I will never make you feel that way. Your virtue is yours until you willingly give it, and no sooner, *ja?*"

"*Ja,*" Freya whispered, her eyes welling with tears. "And for that, I thank you, Soren." She cupped my cheek. "More than you could ever know."

Leaning my cheek into her soft touch, I was about to say more when a soft rap came at the door.

"'Tis food," I murmured. "But it can wait if—"

"No, answer it." She pulled her hand away. "Please. They prepared it and delivered it, so we should be grateful."

Loving her for not just her fierce but soft heart, I nodded and went to the door, allowing the food to be brought in before sitting to eat, only for Freya to surprise me once more. Instead of joining me, she stood, met my eyes, and began undressing not in an adjoining room as she had done thus far but right in front of me.

"I thought, mayhap, before we ate, we might bathe, husband," she said softly, her gaze unafraid as it lingered on me. She removed her boots and trousers, then pulled her tunic off and tossed it aside.

Despite trying to keep my gaze locked on her face, I was helpless to resist taking in all she unveiled, because she was beautiful. Beyond tempting. From the plump roundness of her breasts to the cinch of her waist to the flair of her hips to her long, shapely legs. If that were not arousing enough, she turned and made her way to the tub, allowing me to appreciate her perfectly formed backside before glancing back at me.

"Are you joining me, then?"

Having never heard sweeter words, I followed, shedding my clothing as I went, while she sank into the tub and watched me, not with alarm but with what appeared to be appreciation. Although her cheeks pinkened and her gaze widened ever so slightly when she took in my cock, which was well on its way to being fully aroused, she scooted forward, allowing me to sink into the water behind her.

"Might you unbraid my hair?" she asked, her voice whisper-soft as if she struggled to breathe every bit as much as I did.

"*Ja*," I said, eager to see her hair down once again. To run my fingers through its silky lengths. So, I made swift work of it, captivated by its heavy, vibrant weight in my hands before she dipped beneath the water, then surfaced. After I did the same, she settled back between my thighs and said words I had long wanted to hear.

"I'm not wary of your touch, Soren," she murmured, meeting my eyes over her shoulder. "Not anymore."

CHAPTER ELEVEN
Freya

I T WAS HARD to recall the last time I had such an exhilarating day, from battling with Soren, to being tasked to train his warriors, to finally undressing in front of him and inviting him to bathe with me. Yet we both knew I was inviting him to do much more, and my desire for him only grew when he removed his clothing, revealing an impressive arousal, and climbed into the basin behind me.

My heart pounded wildly as he unbraided my hair, my awareness of him only growing, until I did what I had come here to do. Making myself clear, I looked over my shoulder into his eyes and told him I was no longer afraid of his touch.

"I am ready to become your wife in every sense of the word," I said plainly, if not a little breathlessly.

He searched my eyes. *"Ja?"*

"Ja," I confirmed, unburdened by finally sharing with him the details of my attack years ago. Better still, pleased by his response that he would never do anything I didn't want to do, or ever make me feel so helpless.

Needing no further prompting, he cupped my cheek and closed his lips over mine, kissing me with more passion this time. All the desire we felt for one another roared up, and our kiss deepened. Intensified. Desperate to taste him, our tongues tangled, and I groaned with a mix of approval and need.

Overly aware of his hot, hard length against my backside, a familiar ache blossomed between my thighs, causing me to squirm with want. Seeming to understand what I craved, he continued kissing me while touching me. First, he fondled my overly sensitive breast and pebbled a nipple between his fingers, causing the ache to grow sharper, then trailed his hand down my stomach.

Although I tensed for a moment when he delved into the soft folds between my thighs, I soon relaxed into the immense pleasure of having him touch me there. Rather than growing anxious, I became desperate when the ache intensified into a building sensation that made me move against him and moan.

Once again, seeming to understand what I needed, he trailed his lips down the side of my neck, rolled the pad of his thumb against the nub at the apex of my pleasure, and pushed me over an edge. Having never experienced anything so intensely pleasurable, I gasped and stiffened against him, only to tremble and give in to the waves of sensation crashing over me.

Awash in the ebbs and flows pulsing from my center, I was hardly aware he had lifted me out of the water until he laid me on the plush fur carpet beside the fire. I roused to awareness as his lips found mine again, and he kissed me deeply, touching and stroking me here and there. He kissed and flicked his tongue down my neck and over my breasts until he pulled one of my pebbled nipples into his mouth, making me arch into the vividly erotic sensation.

I was helpless to do anything but bask in all the delicious ways he kept making me feel. The touch of his hands. His breath against my tender, vulnerable skin. And everything only intensified as he continued down my stomach, and over my hips until he spread my thighs and put his mouth where his fingers had been minutes before.

Gasping at how much more intense it felt this time, I thought to stop him, but soon lost myself to the feel of him tasting me in a way I didn't know men tasted women. To the wonderful feeling of him licking and devouring me, causing the sweet ache between my thighs to swell into a heavy throb that would soon take me over that incredible edge again.

"Not just yet," he murmured, denying me it when he came over me, settled between my thighs, and gazed into my eyes. "Soon, though, wife and 'twill be even better this time."

Where I had long thought that when this moment came, I would be frightened or at the very least nervous, when he kissed me and rubbed his heavy ridge against my sensitive folds, I only felt a terrible aching need for him. For how he could make me feel.

"Please," I whimpered hoarsely, shocked I had uttered the word, but I was desperate for more…what came next.

It seemed he was, too, because the next thing I knew, he was gazing into my eyes and slowly pressing into me. Stretching me. Filling me. And while there was a pinch of discomfort at first, it soon gave way to something else entirely. Something so much more consuming and magnificent as he fully seated himself, his eyes adrift in pleasure, before he thrust not quickly, as I had seen some men do, against the sides of buildings or even against trees in the woodland, but slowly.

At least at first.

But then I couldn't fault him for speeding up when I begged for it. Needed more. All he could offer me. The throbbing ache plaguing me had fanned out, filling my entire body with an overwhelming desperation to reach that pinnacle with him. To see and feel him go over that edge, too. When that happened, my own pleasure only seemed to intensify, and I moved with him. Became one with him in a way that had us both groaning with need.

When I wrapped my legs around him, it pulled him even deeper inside me, heightening my pleasure. Beyond desperate for more, I gripped his back and we moved even faster. Thrust harder, hitting a fevered pitch, our skin slick with sweat. Frenzied, crazed with need, we moved until a swelling sensation roared through me. Hitting his peak at the same time, he thrust deep, locked up against me, and released a ragged groan against the side of my neck.

Crying out, I held on tighter, digging my nails in at the feel of him throbbing inside me mixed with a spearing, indescribable, full-bodied sensation that put everything I'd felt to this point to shame. One that went on for some time as our hearts slammed against each other, and we struggled to catch our breath.

Eventually, as if worried he had taken me too roughly, he looked at me with concern and trailed his finger along my jaw. "How do you feel, wife?"

Basking in the afterglow of everything he'd made me feel, only one thing came to mind, so I offered a sleepy smile. "I feel like I will be giving you many strong sons and daughters."

Relief flashed in his loving gaze, and he met my soft smile before rolling off me and pulling me against his side. "I suspect you might be right."

"'Twas good of you to give me time, but now I wonder if I should have made you wait," I murmured, trailing my finger down his chest, growing sleepier by the moment. "Knowing what I know now."

He chuckled, the sound warm and comforting, lulling me to sleep soon after it seemed because when I stirred awake again, I cuddled against him beneath the furs on our bed. Rain fell steadily on the turf roof, and the fire was down to embers.

Or at least it was until my talisman warmed and flames flickered to life.

Caught in a familiar waking dream, I wrapped a fur blanket around my shoulders and drifted to the fire. Captivated by the way the flames moved, I became mesmerized by the vivid crimson and flaming yellows that gradually turned to pale blues and dark greens, swirling within until they formed a pattern.

"A Scottish plaid," I murmured, gazing deeper. Feeling more.

Seeing more, the green became a stone, and the stone became my sister, Astrid's, pale blue eyes staring back at me.

Fearful eyes full of warning.

"What is it, sister?" I whispered, shaking my head. "I don't understand."

She looked past me to where Soren lay sleeping, and I swore I heard her say, "Don't let him go," yet when I looked back at her, she was gone, and fire was nothing more than dying embers again.

"What is it, Freya?" Soren murmured, stirring awake. Alarmed, he came to me. "Are you well?"

"*Ja,*" I said softly, explaining that I had just heard from my sister in Scotland via the flames. "She warned me you should not go." Frowning, I shook my head. "I couldn't say where, yet 'twould only make sense given recent rumors it would be to Scotland."

"'Tis nothing you need worry about at the moment." Soren sighed and urged me to return to bed. "There has been no word yet from King Hákon, so 'tis merely rumor until 'tis more and nothing that need ruin this night."

"Why didn't you tell me of these rumors?" I crawled back into bed with him. "We have talked much, but nothing about that. I had to hear it from Brynhild despite it being something you might have mentioned sooner, given my sister is there."

"Because I didn't want you fretting when oftentimes rumors carried from tribe to tribe with many a tavern in between, can be misconstrued." He tucked me against him. "Rather, I wanted you to enjoy your time getting to know your new tribe whilst you reacquainted yourself with your new husband."

"I would say we have accomplished that," I murmured, finding it challenging to remain frustrated while cozied against him. Before resting my hand on his strong chest, I mistakenly brushed it against his hard arousal, liking the feel of it a great deal now that I knew what it was capable of.

"Mayhap 'twould do us no harm to keep reacquainting ourselves," I went on huskily. Inhaling his spicy, masculine scent, I trailed my fingers downward, only for him to chuckle and rest his hand gently over mine, ceasing its movement. "If you keep going, 'twill be all the harder to deny you, and you need a day or two to heal after this first time, lest it be quite painful the next."

Although my desire had returned along with his, there was a pinch of pain below that told me he was right, so despite how frustrated I was, I heeded him and dozed off again faster than I expected.

Despite my nagging worry, the next day dawned bright and clear, and my new life resumed as usual, only better now that I knew what it felt like to lie with my husband. Moreover, I knew we would do it often once I had healed, and we did. Every chance we got as the days rolled by. Sometimes it was slow and romantic, while at other times it was frenzied and out of control.

And I enjoyed it all every bit as much as he did.

"You are insatiable, wife," he teased one such time when we simultaneously happened by our lodge during the day. Having been desperate for him since the last time we lay together, I yanked him to me the moment the door closed.

"Should I stop, then, husband?" I murmured against his lips as he hoisted me against the door.

"I think the time for asking is past." Just as desperate, he freed himself. "Long past, might it never be asked again."

When he thrust deep, driving me up the door, I nearly howled in pleasure. After that, I was awash in one long, outstanding, never-ending release as he rode me so hard we sailed off the edge together mere minutes later. In fact, it was so intense this time, I swore horns blared in triumph from the great halls of Valhalla.

Unfortunately, I soon realized it wasn't just in my head.

"Hell," he muttered, spilling the last of his seed in me before we adjusted our clothing and he opened the door.

"Who are they?" I asked, dread rolling through me when we spied several ships approaching from the south.

"I could not say from this distance." He pulled a battle axe from the wall and sheathed it at his side. "Grab your shield and blade, and we'll go find out."

Pleased that he wanted me with him, and armed no less, I did as he asked, and we made our way down to the shore, where Ivar stood with several warriors waiting for the ships to get closer.

"'Tis the king's flag flying on one of them," a man called out, and my stomach sank.

They were coming for Soren and his warriors. I was never so sure of anything. Yet I had no choice but to stand with him as they docked and met, who turned out not to be King Hákon himself but one of his top warriors. A man by the name of Leif Olander, who was cordial if not blatant in his admiration of me.

"You are every bit as beautiful as 'tis said, Freya," Leif praised, smiling broadly when Soren introduced us to each other on the pier. "If not younger than I anticipated, given the stories of your battle prowess years ago."

Although slighter in stature than Soren, he was not unhandsome but pleasing enough to look upon, with light blond hair braided back and sharp sea-green eyes. It seems he had met Soren years before, but rarely saw him. There was no missing the cross hanging around his neck, marking him as a Christian.

"How lucky for you, my friend." Leif clasped Soren on the shoulder. "To marry the likes of someone of your wife's ilk, for she is of the bear and a legend along with her sisters, is she not?"

"She is that and so much more." A twinkle lit Soren's gaze when he looked at me, subtly reminding Leif I was his. "She is now trainer to my warriors, the woman who holds my heart, and hopefully soon mother to our strong sons and daughters." He eyed Leif's three ships. "What brings you this way on the king's behest, my friend?"

"'Tis best shared over an ale before a warm fire," Leif said. "It's been a long journey and 'twill be longer still after we leave this stronghold, so good food and company whilst we discuss things would be most welcome, Earl Soren Dahl."

The use of his formal title made me tense. It meant Leif was very much here on behalf of the king rather than for pleasure in passing.

"But of course, Leif," Soren assured, giving orders to his men that they help see the ships properly moored for the eve and that Leif's men were given quarters before joining everyone in the great lodge for food and drinks.

"Very good." Unease flashed in Leif's eyes when he glanced at Sten stalking along beside us. "I see your wolf remains ever faithful, Soren."

"*Ja.*" Lest any of Leif's men admire me overly much, Soren made clear how esteemed I was in these parts, to men and wolves alike. "Ever faithful to both me and Freya, as it turns out, for he rarely leaves her side any more than I tend to these days." He gestured at a lodge just inside the gates used for meetings with those from other tribes to settle business before everyone partook in pleasure. "Come, my friend. Let us speak in there so that I might better understand your arrival."

Leif stopped at the entrance after I followed Ivar and a warrior who was clearly Leif's second-in-command inside, and looked at Soren in confusion. "Surely you don't want your wife here whilst we speak of what I can assure you are important matters of the crown, Earl Soren."

"Of course I want her here," Soren said, making me love him all the more despite having yet said the actual words to him. "We are partners in all things, and I respect her opinion."

Even if it was acceptable to argue my presence, Leif saw as clearly as I that Soren's tone and expression broached no room for argument. So we sat at a table before a crackling fire, and Soren poured everyone ale, urging Leif to share why he was here, and it was just as I had suspected.

Not good at all.

"As you know, King Hákon was most upset by the Scottish invasion of the Isle of Skye last year," he began. "Since then, he's been determined to have his revenge and reclaim more of a

Norwegian presence on the mainland. Land that was rightfully ours for years, claimed and established by our Viking ancestors." He gestured at me, smart enough to include me now. "By shield-maidens of old, such as your lovely wife."

"And how does King Hákon plan to execute this revenge?" Soren perked an eyebrow at Leif. "Better still, where is he now?"

His answer did not surprise me.

It did, however, confirm my fear of the crack in my bow and my sister Astrid's warning from the distant shores of Scotland.

CHAPTER TWELVE
Soren

"KING HÁKON IS heading for the Hebrides with a sizeable fleet that's only going to grow larger," Leif shared as we sat in the lodge we utilized for diplomacy, along with Freya, Ivar, and Leif's second-in-command. "Many are already heading that way, including me and my men after summoning you and as many men as you can spare, Soren, without leaving your stronghold undefended."

There was no need to look at Freya to sense her tension. This aligned with the crack in her boat, destined to divide us, as well as her sister, Astrid, warning her I should not go, having assumed it was to Scotland. And now here I was being summoned to its very shores, and I wanted it no more than she, but if my king called on me, I would go to his aid.

"The king wishes us to leave within the week and meet him in the Hebrides with fresh supplies," Leif went on. "I could not say when he plans to attack, but I suspect 'twill be soon after."

"I have heard much of Scotland's King Alexander III," Freya said. "They say he is fierce and known for his successful military campaigns." She tilted her head in question. "So why would King Hákon risk his countrymen when mainland Scotland is all but lost to us and there are other, less difficult places to conquer?"

While no one would say it aloud, the answer was simple.

Pride.

They had attacked us, and so we would retaliate in kind.

"'Tis not for me to question my king's reasons," Leif said dutifully. "Though I can tell you he has called on some of his fiercest Norwegian tribes, including Soren's, to aid him so there is much hope. Let us not forget, though tribes still war with each other, our king has brought our beloved country far. You recall he was born when our Norway was still torn apart by decades of civil war, *ja?* Since then, 'tis safe to say he's made great strides in the unification of our country and the expansion of our empire."

Even if I agreed with Freya, he was right, so there was no argument here, only acceptance and a focus on what lay ahead. "'Tis early in the harvesting season, so our food storage is low, but we will spare all we can and ready the ships over the next few days for traveling."

"Anything you can spare would be most appreciated," Leif said. "Weapons as well, if you have some to spare."

"We do, but I will have the smithy make more," I replied. "As well as have our hunters gather what furs we can spare for trading."

After Leif nodded in thanks, our business concluded, and we escorted him and his man to their lodgings. I assured them they would receive water for bathing, and we would see them soon to dine, drink, and celebrate the glory of upcoming battles.

As expected, the moment Freya and I returned to our lodge to prepare for the eve, she made her opinion known, none too happy about it, saying everything I knew she would.

"This bodes ill, husband," she warned, her gaze going to the fire as if she saw her sister through the flames even now. "'Tis as the crack in my boat foresaw and Astrid warned, and 'twill be the downfall of many if this happens." She rested her hand over her womb. "Mayhap the ultimate divide betwixt me and you, even as a babe may already grow inside me."

I did not blame her for saying such because it could very well be true, given how often we lay together. Hell, even now, I wanted to carry her to the bed and sink deeply inside her because nothing felt so good.

"Even so." I came up behind her and rested my hands on her shoulders. "You always knew if our king summoned me, I would go. I would have no choice because I love my country." I peppered kisses down the side of her neck. "Almost as much as I love you."

She had yet to return the words, and while I longed to hear them on her lips, I already knew she loved me. It was in every touch. In the way she gazed at me when she didn't think I was looking. It was evident in her words when she worried over me or we laughed together. Even when she grew angry with me, much like she did now, because anger very much simmered in her eyes when she turned and gazed at me.

"These men you will confront in Scotland are not the farmers with pitchforks our ancestors faced, but seasoned warriors. Strategists who are fierce in their need for freedom, not just from us but from the English." She shook her head. "King Hákon's endeavor is truly unwise. 'Twould be like the Scots daring to attack the Norwegian mainland, and you know it."

Rather than acknowledge that I knew she was right, I tried to redirect the conversation. "You know more of Scotland than I realized."

"Then mayhap you don't truly believe I'm in contact with Astrid from afar, however sporadically," Freya returned. "She's shared many things about the land upon which she walks now."

"I *do* believe you," I said softly because I did, just as I believed I brought Freya back from the land of the dead when a child. I could not say how, only that I did. "Just as I believed the gods gifted my mother with the same mystical abilities."

Freya rested her hand on my chest and looked at me with her heart in her eyes. "Then listen to me when I tell you if you go, we might never see each other again."

Resting my hand over hers, I said all I could for now. I reminded her of who she married. Just as I had reminded her who I married when I put a blade back in her hand and asked her to train my warriors to fight as well as her. "'Tis what it must be, Freya. I'm Soren Dahl, 'The Brazon', so I shall be that for my king if he requests it and fight any battle he orders me to. Just as I know you would do the same in my position."

She blinked back tears and turned away to change before I could try to comfort her.

"Then I will go with you and protect you," she vowed, running a comb angrily through her hair. "We will fight these Scots together."

Although tempted to tell her no such thing would happen because I had given my word to her father, I kept quiet for now, having learned to bide my time with her just as she had with me. There were moments to fight and moments to wait. This moment was for peace so that Leif and his men would only see me and Freya unified tonight.

Yet as we prepared and she wove small braids into her hair, opting to present herself as the shield-maiden she was with her white bear cloak, I knew she understood I would not so easily comply later. Yet for now, we went through the formalities of the evening, enjoying good food, mead, and ale to music, merriment, and bards singing tales of old.

"Freya does well this eve despite the storm I sensed brewing betwixt you two," my aunt murmured at one point. We sat at the head table watching Freya mingle with Leif's men. Though ever gracious, she was clearly a warrior born of the berserker with her blade sheathed at her waist, her shield at her back, and a dash of war paint on her delicate face. Brynhild looked at me in warning. "And 'twill not fare well for you because her heartache and anger run deeper than the seas."

"Yet there is nothing I can do to assuage it," I said, downing half my ale.

"You could bring her with you," she suggested, sighing as she watched me clench my jaw. "Yet we both know you will not because your word is worth more than anything." She kept considering me, seeing inside me as only she could. "Or mayhap she is more important than even your word." Her eyes narrowed. "Mayhap not just her."

"There have been changes in her over the past few weeks," I confessed softly, comfortable sharing with my aunt. "Her breasts are fuller and more tender, and her desires are even stronger than usual." I couldn't help but smile a little because my wife was wonderfully lusty indeed. "Which is saying something." Biting back emotion, I could not take my gaze off Freya. "And she has not bled in weeks."

"Sweet Odin in Valhalla," Brynhild whispered. She blinked back tears and looked from Freya to me, squeezing my hand in hope. "Are you sure?"

"*Ja.*" My heart soared at the thought of it, and I squeezed her hand in return. "Whilst I think she suspects it, she doesn't truly know, as this is too new to her."

"Then you should tell her," Brynhild insisted. "It might help her find peace in your absence, for surely she must not leave these shores now."

Although she was right, I feared Freya might not see it that way, and my fears were confirmed a few days later, when the ships were loaded and final preparations were underway for the journey. We would depart at daybreak, and I had yet to make it clear she wouldn't be traveling with me.

She had been cordial to me since Leif's arrival but less warm in our bed, distant in a way that told me my aunt was right. A storm brewed between us that could rain down at any time, so I had to confront it head-on.

First, however, I had to deal with my second-in-command, Ivar, and he would not like it.

"Everything is in order and ready to go," he reported when I joined him at the shore, eyeing the horizon with anticipation. "'Twill be good to battle alongside each other once again for our king, will it not?"

"Come, my friend," I said, heading down the shore away from curious ears. "Let's take a moment alone so that we might talk of things to come."

"Only good things," Ivar said, offering me a rare grin as he joined me.

"To be sure," I agreed, sharing something he would not want to hear any more than Freya would. "With you here protecting what matters most to me because I trust you above all others, Ivar."

When he stopped and frowned in confusion, I stopped too, clasped his shoulder, and met his eyes. "I need you to remain here, not only to watch over our people in my absence but also Freya, for she carries the spirit of the bear and wolf within her womb. She carries my child. This tribe's child."

A variety of emotions churned in his gaze, from frustration to disbelief to hope, which did my heart good, given he had yet to warm to her. "Truly?"

"Aye, truly," I said, never so certain, considering she had grown ill the past few mornings. "So you see why I need you here protecting her." Shaking my head, I could not hide the emotion in my gaze if I tried. "For nothing is more precious to me."

"Nor should it be, my friend," he said, his voice rough with just as much emotion. And though it was hard to agree to this, he did, because we loved each other like brothers. Not just that, but he knew what an enormous responsibility it would be if I did not survive.

"Of course, I will stay and watch over her and your babe with my life if you think it best." Ivar lowered his head in respect. "'Tis a true honor, Soren."

"Thank you." Relieved to hear it, I squeezed his shoulder. "I would also have you two oversee our tribe together in my absence and, worst case, until a new earl is voted in if anything were to happen to me."

He lowered his head again in compliance. "As you wish."

"Very good," I said, pleased to hear it when I thought mayhap this conversation would not go so smoothly. "Then let us return to the village and share an ale before we retire for the eve, for 'twill be earlier than usual."

In agreement, we did just that, laughing and sharing old memories before I sought out Freya. She had been absent for hours now, and I worried about her, yet I sensed she was well enough, and she was. Or should I say she wasn't ill but mayhap not as happy to see me as she might have been when I found her leaning against the towering tree behind our lodge, staring up into the branches swaying in the wind.

Pausing a moment, I admired her red locks flowing down around her shoulders like they had the night we married, and how her crème-colored dress hugged her tempting curves. Her skin was aglow in a new way, radiant in the last soft dewy rays of sunlight cutting down through the leaves, making her appear truly mystical.

"I wondered how long it would take you to seek me out, husband," she said softly, her gaze still trained above until her eyes dropped to me, and I saw not peace within their fiery depths but the shield-maiden come for my warrior's soul. So, when she made a come-hither motion with her finger, I was helpless to do anything but go to her.

Helpless to do anything but let her press me back against the tree, then lower to the ground into a warm patch of grass when she urged me to. Helpless to do anything but watch her hike her skirts and straddle me when I should be telling her how things would be.

Telling her she carried our child.

Instead, when she cupped my cheeks, closed her lips over mine, and ground against me, all I could do was run my hands up her soft, firm thighs and grasp her backside. I had lain with several women over time, including, of course, my late wife, but nothing felt like taking Freya into my arms. Nothing so intense and unforgettable as filling her time and time again, desperate for her even after I'd just had her.

Pulling back, she looked at me without saying a word, freed my cock, and sank onto it so slowly I thought I would die then and there at the incredible sensation of her tight sheath grasping me. Bracing a hand on the trunk beside my head, she fully seated herself, and though her eyelids fluttered and her mouth fell open at her pleasure, she never lost eye contact.

Instead, she shook her head slowly and rode me gently at first, ordering me not to let go too soon, and hell if I didn't comply because she had that kind of power over me. A magical hold that did not let me go as she rolled her hips, bringing me close to peaking before she slowed several times, driving me insane. Eventually, however, it became too much for her as well, because she leaned close and whispered in my ear.

"Do not go, Soren," she pleaded, moving faster as our pleasure built. "Don't leave me and our babe."

Somehow, I wasn't surprised she had figured everything out, but I could not counter her if I tried. All I could do was grip her firm backside and drown in all she made me feel. Sink into her seduction as she continued repeating those words over and over, the faster she moved.

Yet as we peaked at the same time and I wrapped her up in my arms, both of us trembling with the intensity of our release, I knew I had no choice but to leave her and our child safely on these shores. And I found the voice to murmur it in her ear soon after because I had no choice. *We* had no choice. Even if I were not devoted to king and country, saying *no* to King Hákon would turn Norway against our tribe, and I could not have that.

"Nor should you," I said softly, saddened when I finally pulled back and looked at her, only to find her cheeks glistening with tears.

"Did you expect to find anything else?" Freya wondered when I murmured that she should not cry and brushed them away. She rested her hand over her womb and shook her head, pleading with her eyes. "I can't say what will happen, but nothing good will come of you leaving us, husband, and 'tis crucial you believe me."

"So you know about our little one," I said gently, resting my hand over hers.

"*Ja*, I know," she confirmed. "So please don't go."

"Yet I must," I repeated, reminding her of all the reasons why, dropping a soft kiss on her lips, followed by another and another. "And I think deep down you know it."

"I know it could very well mean your death," she murmured against my lips. "That we might never see you again."

"Then let us make this night last," I said between soft kisses. "Let us forget the world around us and be together tonight as man and wife. As dear friends. As lovers and warriors." I deepened my kisses yet still peppered words in between. "As the Norns, Wyrd, and all the gods would have us."

While I thought she would continue fighting me with seduction and words, she ended up doing the last thing I expected.

CHAPTER THIRTEEN
Freya

ALTHOUGH I KNEW Soren expected me to continue fighting him about leaving after we made love beneath the tree out back, I did no such thing. Instead, I brought him to bed and lost myself in his arms for the entire night. We never ate or drank, but made love time and time again until dawn broke, and we made our way down to the sea to watch our last sunrise together.

Somehow, I wasn't surprised it was all the same shades of crimson, yellows, blues, and greens I had seen in the flames the night my sister spoke to me. I said as much, too, before making my way back to our lodge to prepare for his departure while he oversaw final preparations.

Wiping away the last of my tears for now, I braided my hair as I had the day that he'd arrived at my father's holding and painted my face for war because saying goodbye to him felt like going to battle. Then, I adorned the trousers and tunic I had worn the first day I fought him here at our stronghold, wrapped my bear fur over my shoulders, and sheathed his mother's sword at my side.

Holding her shield at the ready like my shield-maiden ancestors and with Sten by my side, I made my way down to the shore with my head held high, pleased when many fell in behind me, understanding the honor I meant to show my husband. The days of our Viking ancestors might have passed, but we still carried them in our blood, and I would see Soren sent off knowing such.

As expected, most at the shore who were preparing to leave stopped what they were doing at my approach, including Soren, and our gazes connected across the distance. As it was every time we looked at each other, I felt the palpable energy of our bond, struggling to imagine it not being a part of my life anymore if something happened to him. Truthfully, I wondered how I ever got by without it to begin with.

"Thank you for this, Freya," he said when he joined me, admiring my appearance. "I'm honored. Might I carry a piece of your warrior spirit with me." Soren looked past me to the villagers who had followed. "Many thanks to all of you for seeing me off."

After saying their farewells to him, he bid goodbye to Ivar and Brynhild, embracing his aunt before slipping his hand into mine so that we might walk to his boat together. Doing my best to keep my emotions reined in, I assessed the numerous ships traveling with him as well as his warriors, and all looked in good form.

"I will miss you more than words can say, wife," he said softly once we arrived at his ship, cupping my cheeks. "Both of you so very much."

"And we will miss you." I rested one hand over our child and one over his heart. "May both of us give you strength and protection wherever you may be, and might our hearts beat as one."

I wasn't surprised to feel my pendant and talisman warm at my chest, telling me great magic was at work in my words. Magic born of the gods that would bind us three, given that his offspring was as mystical as his mother and me.

"I felt that," he exclaimed softly, his pupils flaring with awe. "I felt the warmth beneath your hand pulse and fill me." He closed his eyes for a moment, as if cherishing the sensation, then looked at me again. "'Tis like nothing I have ever experienced."

"'Tis my and our child's love for you, husband," I said just as softly. "Love so great that 'twill stay with you. Protect you in ways born of the gods and could very well bond us through the flames, as I'm bonded to my sisters."

"I can only pray," he said solemnly, then closed his mouth over mine and kissed me one last time. A deep, soulful kiss that ended far too soon as ships were already sailing and his vessel was next to go.

He looked at Sten, who had remained by my side. "Take care of her and our child, my friend, and I will see you all again soon enough."

His thick black pelt rippling in the wind, our wolf looked from me back to Soren, his gaze steady and watchful in a way that spoke to him understanding his master's request. More so, as he remained faithfully by my side when Soren boarded.

Biting back a fresh round of sadness he didn't need to see right now, I held my head high and my shield proudly, walking down the pier as the ship was untied and the sails raised. Soren and I never stopped looking at each other as the wind caught and his boat lurched forward. Instead, I went to the end of the pier and held his gaze until I could barely see his form in the distance, even as all around me went back to their morning duties and routines. I watched him until all I could make out was his ship's sails glowing in the morning sun, until even that disappeared into the horizon.

Only then did a tear slip free, and I realized Ivar and Brynhild still stood beside me, watching our ships in the distance until the last one disappeared.

"He will be all right, Freya," Brynhild said gently, resting a comforting hand on my shoulder. "As you well know, he's a fierce warrior, and now he has more to fight for than ever."

"*Ja*," Ivar agreed roughly, making himself clear when he looked at me with his typical scowl. "And I will see that what he fights for is well-protected." He gestured dismissively at my attire and jerked his head once. "'Twas good to dress as you did today."

Before I could respond, he spun on his heel and strode for the shore.

I shook my head and looked skyward. "What will it ever take to lessen his frustration at me?"

"Actually," Brynhild mused, watching Soren's obstinate second-in-command as he walked away. "I think that might have been him finally starting to warm to you." Her dark blue eye twinkled when she looked at me. "'Twould have been unthinkable for him to compliment you in any fashion mere months ago."

"True," I conceded. "Yet still, 'tis hard to imagine us overseeing this place together." Counting on her, I cocked my head in question. "With your help, I hope?"

"*Ja*, if you like." Wiping away my tears, pride lit her affectionate gaze. "As Soren became more like a son after my sister's death, you are very much like a daughter to me now, Freya, and I will stand by you always, helping however I can."

"Thank you, Brynhild." Pressing my lips together, I fought another wave of emotion. I had very much needed to hear that, given Soren's absence and my own mother's death. "That means a great deal."

Not just that, but knowing she would stand by me if something happened to Soren in Scotland was comforting.

"I thought mayhap we might take your boat out sometime over the next few days?" Brynhild suggested as we headed for shore. "I know you must spend time with our people whilst they adjust to their earl leaving on such a quest, but I think 'twould be good for you once things settle, as I know you favor being on the sea."

"'Twould be most welcome." I managed a wobbly smile for her. Little gave me as much peace and clarity of mind as sailing. "Most welcome, indeed."

"I will see you again soon, my friend and new daughter," Brynhild said once we reached the shore. She squeezed my hand and looked at me with wisdom. "Mayhap to share a cup of ale this first eve alone before you dine with your people?" Her voice grew softer still. Discreet. "Mayhap this first eve without Soren when you pray as you once did?"

"I would like that," I whispered because I couldn't quite find my voice. It seemed Brynhild knew me better than I realized. Knew things even Soren did not.

So, after spending most of the day dressed as I was, a shield-maiden for all to see so they knew I would stand strong for them always, I knocked on the door of a small cottage toward the back of the stronghold, finally ready to embrace another part of me.

My long-abandoned inner seer.

Soren hadn't spoken of it much after I told him I would never divine again after steering my mother wrong, but when he did, it was important to him that I be everything the gods wished of me. Everything my mother would have wanted me to be. He didn't feel that she, nor the gods, blamed me for her death any more than they blamed me for my father's bear mauling and disfigurement.

So, for him and our people, I had met with the seamstress when I knew he would be leaving, determined to honor his wishes and be strong for everyone who depended on me in his absence.

And strong meant being both a shield-maiden *and* a seer.

Strong meant believing in myself and what the gods had gifted me with, praying they would be there for me as I took this first step.

When the village seamstress, a kindly, full-figured young woman with round, rosy cheeks, and a thick crop of dark curls opened the door, I nodded hello and tried to hand her a coin, but she refused it. Saying nothing because she knew I wished this exchange to be discreet until tonight, she gave me a package wrapped in fur.

After handing it over, she offered a small smile, and I smiled in return.

"Please?" I said softly, asking her to place her hand in mine.

"Don't be afraid. I only wish to give you something in return for your kindness and discretion in doing this for me."

Although tentative at first, when I gestured that she could trust me, she slipped her hand into mine and waited as I closed my eyes. Waited as I did something I hadn't done in a long time. Inhaling deeply, I prayed to the gods to flow through me again. Empower me. When my talisman warmed, and I heard the telling whisper of my deities in my ear, I could not help but smile, knowing now that they had never left me. Moments later, warmth spread through me, and my ancestral seer abilities surfaced, filling me once more. I embraced and welcomed them like an old friend I had shunned because I had.

Not anymore, though.

Now I welcomed clarity past the barriers of mortality into something deeply profound and mystically vivid.

Opening my eyes, I offered her a small, knowing smile that she would understand. "Say yes, *ja,* when your friend asks you to marry him because he loves you as fiercely as Earl Soren and I love each other."

The seamstress's hand fluttered to her chest, and her gaze rounded in surprise before a lovely smile blossomed on her face, and she nodded. "Thank you, m'lady."

Lowering my head in acknowledgment of well-received divination, I returned to my lodge, wishing I could run the whole way, and leaned back against the door the moment it shut behind me.

I released a choppy, broken-hearted sigh that I felt like I'd been holding for years. It was the first time I was back here without Soren, and everywhere I looked held a memory. A shared moment. A look of love or desire. Laughter or frustration. Tales of old or new memories just created.

Sinking down against the door to the floor, I held my head in my hands and finally cried. Really and truly wept, knowing I could only do this in private now, as I needed to be strong for our people. Wept for all the moments we would miss while he was away and for those we might never have if he died. I wept until there were no more tears left and rested my head back, eyeing the lodge that would be ours always, whether he returned to me or not.

If I knew nothing else, I would never love nor lie with another if I lost him. My life would become watching over his people and raising our child. Loving him or her for both of us, forever reminding them who their father, Soren Dahl, was, so that he might live on in their hearts.

And I would do that by being everything he had wanted me to be.

So, for Soren and his people, *my* people, I opened my fur package and fingered the robes of my calling for the first time in years. Where most seers preferred black or darker-colored robes, Helvig seers wore white to give thanks to the polar bear spirit that watched over them and shared its strength.

Setting aside my robe, I bathed and cleaned my face of paint, then highlighted my eyes with coal and added fresh black paint. This time, I put the runic symbol of divination on my forehead, then a single line beneath each eye, representing the shield-maiden still within me. After leaving my hair down with a few small braids interwoven, I finally put on my long, white, hooded robe.

Taking a long, cleansing breath, I soaked up the wondrous feeling of wearing it again. The rightness of it. Then I knelt beside my trunk, fished a special pouch of talismans from its lining, and slid it into the pocket in my robe.

Knowing Brynhild would come, I went to the large tree out back, beneath which Soren and I had so recently made love, and lowered to my knees on a soft bed of moss, letting my head fall back so that I might taste the wind and fly among the branches. Among the Valkyries, as I felt them all around me, lifting me in ways most could not feel.

For the first time in far too long, I lowered my head and prayed to all the gods. Truly prayed in a way I hoped echoed through all Nine Worlds to Odin's ears. To Freya's. Loki's. Thor's. To any god willing to listen, that they watch over my child and my husband. My people. Our country.

Eventually, Brynhild arrived and knelt beside me. She lowered her head and recited her own prayers before looking at me and saying, "Give me your talismans and I will weave them into your hair so that they're blessed beneath your tree in the heart of your new home."

I fished the small pouch out of my pocket and gave it to her before we sat facing each other. A small smile curled her lips as she poured its contents into her palm, and no wonder, given she likely recognized a few. A piece of the black runic stone from the hilt of Soren's prized sword. A tiny bone I had found at the base of a tree she had claimed would make a fine ship during our lovely afternoon getting to know one another better. A bear's claw my father once gifted me. A tiny braid made from the hair of Astrid's favorite husky. A chip of wood from the first wooden sword Tove made for me when we were children.

All tokens from memorable moments.

"And this," I said softly after she patiently weaved them into my braids, handing her a small piece of metal shaped like a falcon's feather. "Given to me by my mother for the goddess for whom I was named. She, of not just love and war, amongst other things, to keep me strong always." I lowered my head to Brynhild in acknowledgment of the role she had taken in my life. "Just as you, my new mother, who's still here with me on Midgard, will keep me strong."

Brynhild blinked back tears and nodded, weaving it in with great care as she finalized a return to myself I never thought I would make. Her eyes met mine in equal acknowledgment, and she lowered her head in respect. "Welcome back, Seer Freya Helvig, reborn as Seer Freya Dahl. May the gods watch over you always and shed their light on all the souls you touch."

We lowered our heads in prayer to the gods, then met each other's eyes again.

"'Tis done," I said. Accepted. *Welcomed*.

"'Tis and I have never been prouder, my new daughter." Brynhild clasped my shoulders and grinned, effortlessly going from what my seer needed to what my shield-maiden needed. "Now might we share that ale we spoke of earlier before you go greet your people with all the pieces of your soul intact?"

Feeling a sense of lightness despite my heavy heart, I met her smile with one of my own. "I would like nothing more, my new mother."

So, we did, enjoying an ale in front of the hearth which I had spent many an eve enjoying with Soren, and I was never more grateful for her companionship. Her friendship. Sometimes we chatted and laughed. Other times, I stared into the flames and allowed myself to mourn his leaving.

Yet I never allowed myself to sink too deeply, nor did she.

"Thank you for sharing what will soon be my last ale with me," I said once we finished. "After tonight, I will have river water boiled for me ahead of time and drink it plain or flavored with berries."

When she looked at me curiously, I rested my hand on my womb. "'Twill be better for the babe. Safer. So say the gods."

And they had, though I could not say why, only that it became certain knowledge as I sat before the fire with her.

"As you wish," she said, trusting in my divination. "Then shall we go greet your people anew and share one last ale or mead with them, so that they might know all of you?"

"*Ja*, I would like that very much."

I meant it too, as I pulled on my hood, keeping my talismans visible, and sheathed my blade at my side. Keeping my shield in hand so that everyone might see all of me, I stepped out of my front door for the first time without Soren by my side. Pausing, I caught the eyes of my gray wolf through the fog drifts just rolling in, only for him to vanish a breath later. He had been there, though, and it gave me great comfort.

"Well, then, my friend?" I said, looking at Sten, who sat unwaveringly by the door, keeping guard. "Shall we show them what Soren always saw in me?"

The great black wolf looked in the direction of my wolf as if he saw him too, before he looked at me, and our gazes held in a moment of mutual understanding. That's when I knew what I had always known deep down: my wolf was there but never really there, born of mysticism and destiny, forever just out of reach but always with me as I saw my Wyrd through.

Always watching over me, just as Sten did.

Just as he would going forward, as the Norns and Wyrd did indeed unfold after that, and prophecy revealed itself in truly terrifying ways.

CHAPTER FOURTEEN

Soren

Isle of Arran, Firth of Clyde
Off the West Coast of Scotland
Two months later

EVERY OTHER TIME I left the shores of my stronghold, there had been great anticipation in my heart, whether I was off to battle or otherwise. Yet, as my ship pulled away this last time, that moment of watching Freya stayed with me. Haunted me as my men and I sailed to the Hebrides, then on to Arran with King Hákon. She had never looked more beautiful, standing proudly in her war-paint, holding her shield, her hair blazing like flame in the morning sun, her white bear cloak billowing in the wind.

Since arriving in the Hebrides after an arduous journey, I had wished every moment that I'd not left her and our unborn babe, despite having had no choice. I often thought of the warmth from her touch when she swore the love of her and our child would watch over me via the gods, wishing it would return. Wishing I could feel that mystical bond. The warmth of her spirit.

Yet the days, despite being warmer in the summer months, had somehow seemed colder, and despite her claiming we had mystically bonded, I had not felt that same magical sensation between us that I had on the pier. That sense of rightness.

Rather, everything had felt the opposite.

Although many claimed King Hákon's reign had led Norway into a golden age of sorts, I felt more strongly by the day that his actions in this cause would end in the demise Freya feared. I had grown certain that my king's relentless determination to see through invading Scotland—despite receiving a cool reception from his own Norwegian nobles in the Hebrides—was foolhardy.

"You brood again, my friend," Leif said, joining me in my tent. One of many that were part of an encampment near territories we had been ordered to raid for more supplies.

"As do you," I muttered, having imbibed one too many ales. Gazing at the flames, I wished I were back in my lodge with Freya by my side. "I feel as though my soul has aged years and 'tis…" *What?* I had no words for how I felt other than those. "These are not the battles of old, and you know it." I shook my head. "There is no honor to it anymore. No betterment for our people."

Much had changed, or perhaps become what it always should have been, between me and Leif since leaving the shores of my stronghold. Though we had worked as a team to arrive safely, we had weathered storms and lost men, and once we landed, it was only to find King Hákon a foul beast who often acted irrationally in his need for revenge. He was in such an unstable mood these days that Leif and I teamed up frequently to figure out how to see through his erratic orders without causing too much unnecessary harm.

Orders that neither of us agreed were worthwhile anymore.

Initially, I was wary of Leif's motives, as he was one of Hákon's top warriors and his longtime friend, that is until he lost nearly all the men he'd traveled here with, friends all, to an ambush. One that Hákon said would not happen, despite Leif's protests that it very well might, and it had changed his viewpoint significantly after that.

Leif poured an ale, sat beside me in front of the fire, and sighed. "Whether there is honor or not, we are the king's men, and so we must rally on."

"Rally on when we fight a losing battle, and you know it."

Frowning, I shook my head, my gaze never leaving the fire in hopes that Freya somehow reached out to me via the flames.

"Yet still," Leif said softly, sounding as defeated as I. "He is our king, Soren, and will need us to do something in a few days."

I closed my eyes before narrowing them at my friend. "What *this* time? Because I grow tired of taking from people who did me no harm. People who do nothing more than farm the land and try to survive, like me and my tribe. Your tribe. Tired of fighting without a cause because it does not exist here anymore." Downing the last of my ale, I shook my head. "Our king has brought our country far, but we're not there yet. Now is the time to squelch the strife within our own borders and unify lest we go the way of the Scottish clans. Though they fight well for their freedom, if they don't stop squabbling amongst themselves, they will someday fall to England. Mark my words."

"On that we agree," he murmured, downing nearly all his ale in one long swig before his gaze settled on the flames. "Nevertheless, we have received word that although the Norwegian and Scottish embassies have fiercely debated the sovereignty of the Isles of Clyde, 'tis not going well. Our king is dispatching a fleet to raid into Loch Lomond to ravage Lennox. Meanwhile, we will reposition ourselves between the Cumbraes and the Ayrshire coast."

"Loki's cock," I cursed, pouring myself another ale. "King Hákon means to see through this invasion no matter what."

"*Ja*," Leif confirmed. "And he wants us lying in wait off the Cumbraes as he considers us amongst his best."

Hanging my head, I sent up a prayer to the gods and took several more swigs of ale. "And then?"

"And then, once given the order, we make landfall and secure the area so that the main fleet can follow without a potential ambush."

"So, a stealthy yet not so stealthy approach," I said dryly. "Onto land heavily scouted by seasoned Scottish warriors in no mood to give up their territory any more than I would be, trying to conquer a people already dealing with the English and their endless prodding at Scottish borders."

"You are beginning to sound like a sympathizer," Leif said softly.

"I am starting to sound like the man I have always been," I countered. "One who recognizes a battle already lost, who doesn't want to spill more Norwegian blood over a lost cause."

"So mayhap that is why you and I are here in this moment, my friend," Leif countered, despite the angst in his voice, telling me he loathed it just as much. "Mayhap your gods and my God have sent us so that we might prevent it and see our men safely from Scottish shores in the end."

"Now *that* is the soundest thing I've heard in some time," I admitted. What else was left in this farce of an invasion but to save as many of my countrymen as I could?

"Then let us share another ale and go forward with that in mind." Leif held out his hand to me. "Let us fight as brothers and keep our countrymen safe."

I clasped his hand. "Always."

"*Skald.*" He tipped his glass to me. "To all that will matter in the end."

"*Skald,*" I echoed softly when it usually would be a boisterous toast to men I needed rallied to my cause. Now it was an alliance to keep them safe with no reward. "To all that matters."

As it turned out, we disembarked with four ships two nights later and anchored off the coast of the Cumbraes as ordered. Two of my ships and two of Leif's.

"'Tis not a good day for this," I had warned Leif before we set sail, eyeing the red skies. Nothing good ever came of seeing such before sailing, as it usually preceded bad weather.

"I agree," Leif replied. "But 'tis the king's orders." He shrugged and grinned at me. "I cannot see it being much worse than what we faced sailing around Scotland, and we survived."

"True," I conceded, never one to worry overmuch about a storm, but the air felt different, and the winds shifted too much, making navigation tricky when we set out. Lowering our sails, we took to rowing against choppy waters and higher waves than I would have liked.

The king had decided he wanted us to go ashore tonight under the cloak of darkness to scope things out. He and his fleet would join us the next day.

By the time we arrived, the wind had picked up considerably, and the waves were too big to make it safely past the breakers. Even dropping anchor might prove perilous, but we had little choice.

Thunder boomed, white hot lightning flashed, raging waves battered our hulls, and icy rain sliced down as we tried to keep our ships afloat. It eventually got so bad I could no longer make out the other boats in the rapid lightning flashes, and my heart sank.

"Where did they go?" one of my men roared, trying to be heard over the violent storm.

Shaking my head, I ordered them to tie off or hold onto anything they could because the anchor was doing no good, any more than I suspected it had for the other ships.

A lightning flash later proved it.

"Hell, *streð mik*," I cursed.

Teetering dangerously on its side, one of the other boats was being dragged to shore by angry waves. I wiped rain from my eyes and tried to keep it in sight, but moments later, a wave crashed into our boat, so high that it lolled heavily to one side. Heart pounding, I wrapped my arm around the slick mast and held on tight, thinking only of Freya and our child. I envisioned her luminous amber gaze and the feel of her warmth in my arms while trying to grab one of my men before he went over, but it was too late.

For all of us, it turned out, because the next thing I knew, my ship rolled and I was underneath the frigid water. Pushing off the mast, I dove down and swam with all my might to get clear of my boat as waves kept tossing it closer to the shore. All I could do after that was attempt to make it to shore, too, without drowning in the merciless, raging, wrathful sea.

Finally, and with the gods' help, I found and broke the surface of the water where I struggled to breathe around mouthfuls of salt water. Still, I needed to figure out which way was which in the cloying darkness. Between the rain and the sea, water came at me from every direction, and I lost all sense of bearing until I swore I heard Freya's voice on the howling winds telling me to look for her wolf.

Look for Largs.

It took me a moment to realize she must be speaking of Largs, Scotland. As if to confirm my thoughts, her familiar warmth spread through me, and wolf eyes appeared in the darkness.

"I see it," I gasped.

Finding a fresh burst of strength, I headed in that direction, unwilling to give up. Unwilling to die tonight and never meet my child. Never see my beloved wife again. So, I swam and struggled, and by the grace of the gods, I finally made it to shore, as did many of my and Leif's men.

Better still, despite being battered, all four boats.

When I spied someone struggling to tread water nearby, then slipping beneath the sea, I dove back in and grabbed him. He was older and dressed like a merchantman, no doubt from another ship that must have gotten caught in the storm. His skin was turning blue, telling me he had taken in too much water and wasn't breathing, so I turned him on his side and slammed my hand against his back, hard, glad when he coughed out a mouthful of water.

"Are you all right?" I yelled, trying to be heard over the booming storm. Although he gasped and sputtered, his color was returning.

When he nodded *yes*, I resumed helping as many men as I could, urging everyone to take shelter beneath the trees. We would try to pull the ships ashore once the weather settled.

Scanning the coast for Leif, I was relieved to see him stumbling onto the rocky terrain nearby.

There was no sign of Freya's wolf, but then why would there be when it would have been impossible for him to be here? Somehow, if only in spirit, she had sent him to see me safely to shore. I was sure of it.

Not just me, either, as it turned out.

When I spoke with my men as we waited out the storm, they claimed they, too, had been led to shore by a wolf. Although I could tell they thought it odd, stranger tales had come out of seafarers, and in this case, it saved them.

"Let's see what we can salvage of our boats," I said grimly once the weather finally improved. It was doubtful they were seaworthy anymore, leaving us in a particularly vulnerable position. Scanning the area around us, I saw no immediate threat, so we headed that way.

"Where do you think we landed?" Leif wondered.

"Luckily enough, precisely where King Hákon wanted us to, in Largs, Scotland," I said, continuing to take in our surrounding area and how suited to a battle it might be.

Leif's eyebrows swept up. "How can you be so certain?"

I winked at him. "Because I'm married to a seer, my friend." Grinning, I gestured out to sea and the Norwegian ships on the horizon. "And there you have it. She was right, and we will soon have backup."

"'Tis good, too," one of my men warned, evidently spotting trouble seconds before an arrow whizzed by Leif's head. "Because we have company."

Seconds later, another arrow sliced through the throat of one of Leif's men, killing him instantly. Another landed in one of my men's thighs, and he dropped to his knees. Roaring for everyone to take shelter behind the nearest wreckage, I half-dragged, half-carried him behind the closest boat, which, as it happened, was a merchant vessel, so it must have belonged to the merchantman I'd pulled from the water the night before.

"There," Leif called out, pointing at a band of Scots on a sizeable mound to our northwest. "'Tis coming from there."

Cursing under my breath, I ripped a piece of material off my tunic and pressed it into my man's wound to slow the blood flow after he yanked the arrow free. We had nothing with which to defend ourselves, so all we could do was seek shelter until they got closer, then battle with our bare hands. Even though I spied one or two armored helmets washed ashore, they were inaccessible at the moment, and I had yet to see any weapons.

"They come fast!" Leif gestured at the incoming boats. "We need only hold our ground until then."

They were indeed coming fast, and our fellow countrymen were already jumping ashore by the time the Scots got closer. Realizing how vastly outnumbered they were, the enemy fled before they could cause any more damage.

"Our luck seems to be holding on but by a thread," I muttered to Leif as more Norwegians came ashore soon after, including a wiry but seasoned warrior and nobleman named Ogmund Crouchdance. King Hákon often called on him to command his armies, and this time was no different.

"'Tis good to see you and most of your men alive," Ogmund said in greeting, assessing the wreckage. "King Hákon and the rest of his fleet should be here within the hour." Taking in our surroundings, he pointed to the mound on which the Scotsmen had recently stood. "We will bring a quarter of our men up there, and King Hákon and the rest of the fleet will fight down here, as I suspect we can count on far more Scottish arriving soon."

In agreement, we were given blades, shields, and helmets, and helped prepare with the smaller fleet on the mound. We saw the king sparingly after he arrived, as he oversaw the bulk of his men on the shore. Only long enough to offer his condolences on the loss of our men's lives, and to assure us he would see our ships replaced. It was more than most kings would do, so we could only be grateful, despite how foolhardy we still thought this venture.

Unfortunately, late in the afternoon the next day, our run of questionable luck ran out when a sizeable Scottish force approached not from the north or east as Ogmund and King Hákon thought they would, but from the south. That meant they could very well cut our smaller fleet off from the shore, which, far outnumbered, would lead to our inevitable slaughter.

"'Tis a sizeable vanguard," Ogmund's scout reported, seeming distressed and rightfully so. "Mayhap double our entire fleet and well-armed."

Leif and I glanced at each other as Ogmund debated how best to handle this. We knew there was only one course of action if any of us on the mound hoped to survive. We needed to get to the shore with the remainder of the fleet and protect King Hákon as he retreated to safety, for as we'd feared from the start, this was no winnable battle.

When Ogmund continued weighing his options and consulted with us, I said as much. "'Tis not worth it." I looked at him gravely. "Even if by some stroke of luck, we managed to defeat an army twice our size, you can guarantee there will be plenty more behind them, and we'll be too worn down at that point." I gestured at the ships in the distance. "Our wisest move to spare countless lives is to leave now, whilst there's still a chance."

"I agree with Soren," Leif said. "'Tis the soundest course of action."

Ogmund considered us for a moment before, thankfully, he conceded and ordered all to begin an orderly trek down the mound back to the oceanfront.

"Now let us hope 'tis not too late," I said under my breath, striding alongside Leif. A bad feeling churned in my gut despite our promising course of action. Yet all seemed to be going well as we made our way through the woodland and twilight descended.

That is, until several arrows came out of nowhere and two men fell.

"Here we go again," I muttered before the forest erupted behind us with Scottish warriors who knew this land far better than we did.

Spinning, I whipped a dagger into a warrior flying at me on horseback, then spun and drove my blade into the shoulder of another as the woodland exploded in battle around me. Dropping to a knee when two more came at me, I sliced the calf of the Scot on my right and spun low, tripping the other. When he hit the ground, I pressed my heel to the back of his neck and drove the same dagger into his shoulder, causing a great deal of pain and rendering his arm useless.

"Go," I roared at Ogmund.

Leaping to my feet, I whipped another dagger, dropping a man who had rushed at my commander from behind. Though it broke my heart to say it because I knew I would never see Freya again nor meet our child, I would protect my king and as many of my countrymen as possible. "Lead as many as you can to the shore and see him safely from these shores, Ogmund." I looked at my men, not wanting them to die so pointlessly either. "Go!"

I had purposely not said Hákon's name to Ogmund so the Scots wouldn't know they fought the King of Norway himself. Nodding once at Ogmund in reassurance, I let him know I intended to hold back as many Scots as I could to give him and as many of our men as possible a chance to flee.

Then, I turned, battle axe in hand, ready to face off with too many warriors to count, only for everything to still inside me for a flicker of a moment. Calm in a way I had never felt before, Freya's warmth filled me, and I knew she was with me somehow in these final moments.

As if time had slowed, I looked to my right and saw the spirit of a large blackish-gray wolf, representing my ancestors, and to the left, a monstrous polar bear, representing hers. Here at Freya's command to lend me strength. Courage. Ferociousness. Fearlessness. Empowered by it, battle lust overcame me, and I raced toward a wall of warriors.

It became a battle dance of rage and blood after that, as I fought dozens, only to realize I was not alone. Leif was beside me along with several of my men, and we fought as a team. We spun, sliced, kicked, and punched, fighting more than we could ever conquer while buying our countrymen time.

Yet as we fought, we fell one by one.

First one man, then the next, then another, to the mighty power of the Scots defending their land, and I felt the loss of my men to the core. Mourned them even as I roared and kept battling, relentless in my need to save as many as possible, may they soon be offshore.

Then it was just me and Leif, with far too many coming at us.

We worked together, fighting the best battle of our lives, cutting down enemy after enemy until so many came at us that I lost sight of him in the mayhem. At one point, I thought I glimpsed him going down, but I had no way of helping him with so many coming at me.

After that, everything seemed to go by slowly and fast all at once, as I battled on and on until someone slammed me onto my back. The air rushed from my lungs, and I tried to move, fight back, anything, but it was too late. A Scottish warrior stood over me with fury in his eyes and drove a broad sword into my gut, roaring, "Heathen!"

Then he was gone, and all I could do was watch helplessly as endless Scots rushed by me toward the shore.

Staring up at moonlight cutting through swaying branches, I heard the clashing of metal in the distance and the roars of battle before everything quieted, leaving me with the sound of the wind. I felt its cool caress against my cheek and the warm blood trickling from the corner of my mouth.

"Freya," I tried to call out so that she might hear me from the distant shores of my homeland, but I could not speak.

All I could do was stare up into the trees and wait to join my kin and friends in the great halls of Valhalla, yet instead I saw the face of a wolf staring down at me, then that of a polar bear, then Freya.

Here.

With me somehow.

Lifting my hands, I tried to caress her cheeks one last time. Feel her soft, silky skin. Tell her how much I loved her. Yet before I could, she faded, and I knew it was too late.

I drew in one last breath, and all went very, very dark.

CHAPTER FIFTEEN
Freya

"DO NOT LEAVE us," I wailed, jolting awake.

In a cold sweat of panic, I sat up and tried to get my bearings. Though I had felt like I'd been in a chilly, dark forest moments before, I was still in bed in mine and Soren's lodge. Wind howled, and waves crashed in the distance just as they had moments ago in my dream.

Yet it had felt so real.

Powerful.

Heart-wrenching.

Putting a hand to my womb, I knew our babe was safe. It had been something else.

Soren.

I was sure of it.

Compelled, I slipped into my night rail, wrapped my bear fur around me, drifted out to our tree, and stared up at the moon-light pouring down through its branches.

Since I had embraced my gift two months ago, my powers of divination had only grown stronger. Clearer. Especially when I dreamt, giving me insight into things to come, or sometimes as they were happening in another location.

"Soren," I whispered, murmuring prayers to the gods.

"Where are you, my love?" I dropped to my knees in supplication to my deities but never stopped looking up. "Talk to me. *Be* with me."

Over the past few nights, my pendant and talisman had remained warm against my skin, telling me we were connecting, despite the distance. However, there was a chill between us born of the unease Soren felt wherever he was. A mental wall that made it hard to bond with him, yet last night I had awoken in a panic, much like how I woke tonight.

Last night, I had dreamt of my gray wolf and a raging storm at sea. Of ships rolling and men crying out. Of *Soren* crying out. Fearing for him, for all of them, I had beckoned him, *them*, to come to me. Come to the wolf, and find the safety of the shore.

Now tonight, the feeling was so much more intense. Vivid. Fast, furious, and relentless, as though the storm of nature became a storm of warriors. Staring down at my hands, I saw an axe in one hand and a dagger in the other. Felt warm blood speckled on my face and neck as I poured myself into Soren's heart in a way that felt truly otherworldly.

Looking to my left, I saw the spirit of a polar bear. To my right, the spirit of a wolf. Then, I felt only my ancestral berserker and a vicious need to protect my countrymen and king. To give them a chance to flee.

"Fight," I roared as the wind whipped up and the tree branches above bent and swirled. "*Fight*, husband!"

Although terror filled me as Soren fought valiantly and neared Valhalla's great halls, soon to dine with the All Father himself, I stood with him, empowered him, *loved* him, every step of the way.

"No," I wailed when piercing pain sliced through my gut, and I fell back.

I tried to keep wailing, but all went silent, except for the sound of men fighting in the distance, then even that faded, leaving only the wind in the trees and moonlight dancing down through its branches.

"Soren," I whispered, my voice hoarse with emotion as I saw him reaching down to me. Or was he reaching up? It was impossible to tell.

"Do not go," I cried, roared, wailed. "Do not leave me!"

Yet as I reached for him, he faded, and I saw the white furred, blue-eyed face of one of Astrid's huskies peering back before I saw my sister's face and heard her single, mournful, urgent plea.

"Come now, sister! Come before 'tis too late!"

Then her cry became Ivar's roar, and everything snapped away except the angry face of Soren's second-in-command, his dark eyes blazing at me as if he had come for my soul.

Confused, I blinked and tried to get my bearings, only to find myself not kneeling but standing beneath my tree with Ivar's hands on my shoulders as if he had been trying to rouse me awake. Sten released a long, mournful howl from beyond my front door as if he, too, had been trying to get through to me.

While I wish I could say things had improved between Ivar and me since Soren's departure, he only seemed to grow more frustrated and despondent with me the longer Soren was gone, as if I were somehow to blame for it.

So imagine my surprise when his angry scowl turned to a look of relief, and he murmured a prayer of thanks to the gods before speaking more civilly than I expected. "Are you with me now, Freya?" He glanced from Brynhild, who had at some point arrived, too, back to me. "With us?"

"I am," I whispered hoarsely, my throat bone dry as if I'd been screaming endlessly, and it turned out I had been. Enough to rouse many, including Ivar and Brynhild.

"Here," Brynhild said gently, lifting a cup of water to my mouth when she saw how badly my hands shook. "Drink, daughter."

So I did, grateful for the cool water sliding down my parched throat before swallowing hard and continuing to gain my bearings.

"What is it?" Brynhild asked, trusting in my powers of divination as much as everyone else after the past few months. "What did you see? You were calling out for Soren, and it didn't sound good."

"I have to go to him," I managed, relieved to find my voice working again, if not wobbly with emotion. Looking from Brynhild to Ivar, I made myself clear. "My sister told me to, and so I will because Soren is…"

"What?" Brynhild prompted when I trailed off.

I shook my head, unsure yet certain of my path. "Dead…but not dead.

"Which is it?" Ivar bit out, as disgruntled as I and Brynhild. "Where is he?"

"Where I'm going," I made clear again, pulling away and striding inside with them fast on my heels. "And don't try to stop me."

"Yet we will," Ivar growled. "Because you carry Soren's child."

"And *my* child," I growled right back, snagging a dagger from the wall and spinning on him. Though he towered over me, I stood on my tiptoes, went nose to nose with the brute, brought my dagger to his throat, and glared at him. "We are going to save her father, and my husband just as he would for us, and I *dare* you to try to stop us, Ivar. I dare you to stop two Helvig Dahl shield-maidens because we *will* drop you to your knees here and now."

Well aware I held my well-sharpened blade against a vein that would kill him if I sliced, Ivar didn't tremble in fear. Instead, he narrowed his eyes in return, before surprising me again when the corners of his mouth rose a mere fraction and his voice softened. "'Tis a daughter? Truly?"

I couldn't help a small smile in return, because though my belly had barely swelled, I often saw her in my dreams. "*Ja*, she is a beautiful, strong, willful daughter who will kill you herself the moment she can wield a blade if you don't allow us to go to her father's aid this very night."

"No doubt she will if she's anything like her mother," Brynhild said, her voice shaky with emotion at the news because I hadn't even told her yet. She rested her hand on Ivar's shoulder. "So mayhap we should hear Freya out, my friend, for if anyone has proven she possesses the power of the gods over the past few months, 'tis her and it has only been for the betterment of our people."

"It has, and you know it." I pressed my blade tighter against his neck. "So you decide, Ivar. Will you hear me out and allow me to leave, or will my daughter and I end you here and now?"

Thinking about it, Ivar's nostrils flared, and his gaze remained narrowed on me before he relented through clenched teeth, "All right, Freya." His voice softened once more. "If 'tis you and your daughter's wish, I will hear you out."

"Then let us leave," I reiterated. "Because that is the only option and soon."

"Leave when you were honored by your husband to watch over his people," Ivar reminded, choosing to use words and guilt rather than weapons. Not altogether unwise, given his current position.

"Yet would it not be watching over Soren's people if Freya saved him and brought him home alive to watch over them always?" Brynhild said, keeping her voice gentle. "You and Freya have trained excellent warriors to be ever better since Soren left, so 'tis safe to say they can protect themselves and our people in both of your absences with me watching over them."

"Yet I, too, was tasked to watch over our people," Ivar countered.

"As was I," Brynhild pointed out. reminded. "Yet you were also tasked to watch over Soren's wife and unborn child, and you're much better with an oar than I these days." She gave Ivar a look. "You are the better, more formidable choice betwixt us to see Freya safely to Soren's side, and you know it."

"This is no easy journey," Ivar warned me. "Are you sure you want to put your daughter at risk like that?"

"She will not be at risk if she's safely inside me," I made clear.

"And not only is my ship new and built well, but I excel on the sea. We need but six strong oarsmen with us, and we will travel swiftly, reaching western Scotland within the week."

"'Tis swift indeed," he returned dubiously. "And only if you're lucky enough to have the wind at your back the entire time."

"I will be," I lied because I had no way of knowing that. "I would not have heard my sister's call otherwise."

"And what do you intend to do once we arrive?" Ivar wondered. "Do you know where your sister is? Will we be safe going ashore? Somehow I doubt it."

"*Ja*, I know where she is," I assured. "'Tis not all that far north of Largs." Growing tired of this conversation and the time it wasted, I arched an eyebrow and cocked my head. "Come or do not come, but I need to know you will let me go save Soren."

Ivar considered me for a stretch, debating before he sighed and agreed. "Fine, I will allow you to leave these shores and will get you there safely."

I narrowed my eyes in question, wanting to trust him. "*Ja?*"

"*Ja.*"

Now it was my turn to consider him before deciding he told the truth and lowered my blade. Moving right along, I began packing a few things in a satchel and suggested that Ivar go pick the men he felt best suited to our journey.

"I will see to food and boat preparations for a long journey," Brynhild volunteered, and both left to see to their tasks.

After braiding my hair and dressing warmly in trousers and a woolen tunic with my bear fur, I sheathed several daggers, my sword, and shield, and headed down to the shore with Sten by my side.

"Will you be coming all the way to the land of Scots, then?" I asked him. Naturally, he didn't answer, but I suspected he would if it meant bringing Soren home or, mayhap, protecting me and my child as his master had requested.

I was glad to see that both Ivar and Brynhild moved right

along, and we were ready to set sail within the hour. Ivar had chosen good men, and my boat had plenty of provisions, including ample weapons.

"When they rise, tell our people we will bring their earl home safely," I told Brynhild while saying our goodbyes. "They have my word."

"I will." She embraced me tightly. "Take care of yourself, daughter." Meeting my eyes with pride, she blinked back tears. "And stay strong always."

"I will," I assured, because I had to for Soren's sake, more certain of it by the moment.

We set sail shortly thereafter to calm seas and swift winds that were indeed at our back, allowing us to travel quickly. Once again, favoring our journey, the sun rose bright and warm, and we took turns doing various things, from manning the rudder and rowing to handling the sails throughout the day. Although I had never traveled this route, the men had, so they knew which direction to take. Everyone took shifts sleeping to conserve strength, and by the third night, we had settled into a pattern, and all were impressed with how quickly we continued to travel, including Ivar.

"I will admit to doubting your claim that this would happen," Ivar said, joining me at the bow. He handed me some dried meat and cheese. "Though 'tis safe to say your boat must take some of the credit. 'Tis truly a fine vessel."

"It is." I looked at it with pride. "Brynhild is very talented."

"*Ja*," Ivar agreed, taking a swig from his skin of mead before considering the horizon. Although I would not call him warm toward me, there seemed to have been some thawing between us since leaving.

"Against the odds, we should see Scotland's northern isles sometime tomorrow," he went on, shaking his head. "I don't think I have ever heard of anyone making this journey so swiftly."

"No, I can't imagine you have," I said softly, running my fingers along the crack Soren and I were so worried about, feeling a warmth in it this time that made me smile. It was the same warmth I had felt when I bonded with Soren on the dock before he departed. Warmth that told me the gods favored this ship as they favored our union. "But then most boats don't have such talented sailors, nor the power of the bear and wolf at their back."

"Literally on one count," Ivar noted, eyeing Sten, who sat nearby, staring ahead as if he knew we drew closer to Soren. Ivar's attention returned to me, and his voice grew gruff, as if he struggled with his question, no doubt because he wasn't used to behaving civilly to me.

"How do you fare, Freya?" he said. "Is the babe well?"

"Both of us are," I assured him, assuming he was finding some roundabout way to once again grumble about my determination to do this. "No need to concern yourself. As you've already seen, I won't be a burden on this journey."

"I *have* seen," he conceded. "And you sail well." Chomping on a piece of bread, he considered me for a moment as if debating whether to go on or not. "I didn't ask because I thought you were a burden, but because you carry my friend's child and because Soren cares a great deal for you. 'Twould be something he would want asked in his absence."

"And what of you, Ivar?" I wondered, wanting to at last understand his behavior toward me. Better yet, understand how he could blame me for things that were out of my control. "Is it something *you* want to know? Though 'tis hard to imagine, given your clear dislike of me, for things that weren't my fault. Things that were taken out of my hands by illness and my father."

"'Tis true enough," he granted, revealing his point of view, as he gazed out over the moonlit sea. "Even so, that didn't change how sad Soren was when you left after your illness, never even bothering to write him as time went on. After what happened, he'd thought your friendship was unbreakable and would only grow. Then, when his father tried for your hand in marriage at his request years later, 'twas said you rejected him." He shook his head. "We were never told 'twas your father behind it."

"I could see how that would be hard." Noting the sadness for Soren in his dark eyes, I considered him in a new light. "Especially for his closest friend."

"'Twas not easy," he confessed, sighing. "Then I cannot say I was all that impressed when years later, I was under the impression you finally agreed to marry Soren merely because he was renowned now when he was always renowned to those who cared most about him." His gaze settled on me. "Most especially, I would have thought, to the young sick girl he brought back from the brink of death and clearly adored if you but paid attention."

"Now you know I was either ignorant or without control of all of those circumstances." I tilted my head in curiosity. "Should I assume, then, that you were just waiting for me to break his heart all over again since marrying him? Or is there something else we need settled so we might find a friendship? A sense of camaraderie that would please Soren greatly?"

"'Twould not be the first time I saw him rejected within a marriage," Ivar muttered. "So *ja*, I have feared it could very well happen again, given I thought you'd already rejected him several times over." He shook his head again. "And such from you within a marriage would have broken him. 'Twould have been one step too far." He paused a moment, considering things before shrugging and finally consenting. "So 'tis fair to admit it has been difficult to push past my preconceived notion of you…until now."

"Why now?"

"Need you ask?" For the first time since we met, he looked at me with pride and approval. "Now you have very much proven there is no length you won't go to keep him safe. Protect him. And that—" he gestured at my boat—"*this*, what you are determined to do at significant personal risk, shows me how much you care about him. And that is all…"

He trailed off when a heavy gust of wind blew up out of nowhere, and the boat lurched forward so fast the oarsmen had to lift their paddles.

"Oh no," I whispered, murmuring a prayer to the gods when the ocean grew darker around us, and I felt the ominous presence of the land of the dead, yet knew it didn't cast its shadow on me, but my other half.

Soren.

Blinking back tears and trying to appear strong when I felt anything but, I rallied those sleeping to wake. We needed to put all oars in and row even faster than the winds that were carrying us.

"If we do not, we will lose Soren before we reach him," I warned, fearing it might already be too late.

CHAPTER SIXTEEN
Soren

EVEN AFTER BEING immersed in eternal darkness after getting cut down in Largs, I longed for Freya and our child, when I should only be eager to visit the great halls of Valhalla now. To finally share an ale with my All Father. Yet the darkness did not fade, and I feared I was in Hel, the land of the dead despite dying honorably in battle.

Moments later, the darkness splintered into fragments of shearing pain and moonlight, then all went dark again before I woke to more splintering pain and blinding candlelight. Unable to do anything but moan in agony, I squeezed my eyes shut, only vaguely aware of voices, before fading into darkness once again. The next time I stirred to semi-awareness, men speaking with Scottish burrs were arguing, and a cool cloth pressed to my head.

"Shh," said a gentle, feminine voice with a Norse accent. "'Twill be all right, but you must battle the darkness, Soren Dahl, because your fight is by no means over."

"Where am I?" I rasped, my throat parched and my vision blurry when I cracked my eyes open again.

"Nowhere you want to be, heathen," a deep voice growled. "Nowhere you—"

"Enough," the female interrupted him, a frown evident in her voice. "Now is not the time."

"'Twill soon be, though, lass," he muttered, "because I dinnae like this one bit and he will know it."

"I'm fairly certain he already does," she cut back. "Now, both of you leave us be so that he can be tended in peace. He earned it, did he not?"

"Och," the man grumbled. "He earned nothing but—"

"Go," she bit out more firmly, the octave of her voice reminding me much of Freya's when she grew exasperated, determined to have her way. And I could only be grateful because I was clearly in enemy territory and at the mercy of a man who did not like me.

Where was I, though? Given the woman's accent, I could only pray I had somehow ended up in the hands of Freya's sister, Astrid. Fortunately, once a door slammed shut, implying we were alone, she confirmed it.

"You must try to drink some water, Soren," she said softly, tilting something to my lips. "'Tis crucial so that you see my sister, Freya, once more, for she worries about you greatly and is coming for you."

"No," I tried to say, but cool, refreshing water had already slid down my dry throat, and I had no choice but to swallow, craving it more than I realized.

After gulping down as much as I could before my pain became too much, I must have passed out because when I stirred awake, I was finally able to open my eyes and see my surroundings. I appeared to be lying on a bed beneath fur blankets in a stone room with sparse yet well-built furnishings and narrow windows. A fire burned on a sizeable hearth, telling me I was likely in a castle, and its master was someone of higher rank in their society.

"Good morning," came that same soft, feminine voice, and I realized a woman sat beside me. What looked much like a white wolf with the same pale blue gaze as hers sat by her side. Lovely with honey blond hair tied back and a simple brown linen dress, she smiled and pressed a cool cloth to my forehead once more. "My name is Astrid Helvig, sister to your wife, Freya. Mayhap she has told you of me?" She gestured at the wolf beside her. "This is my husky, Oksana."

I recalled Freya talking about Astrid's huskies. How she ended up with several strays when a child near the Russian border, and now had one of their descendants here in Scotland with her.

"Of course, Freya mentioned you," I managed, my voice still raspy. Despite doing my best to smile, I suspected it didn't quite meet my eyes. The pain in my midsection was still too intense. "She speaks highly of you and your sister, Tove, and misses you both greatly. 'Tis good to meet you, Astrid."

"You as well, Soren, and I miss my sisters just as much." Sadness flickered in her gentle gaze. "Very much."

"What happened?" Frowning when I recalled her mentioning Freya coming to me, I shook my head, hoping I had misheard. "I thought you said Freya was coming, yet I assume I'm somewhere in Scotland despite thinking I died in battle?"

"You are at Mackay Castle on the western shores of Scotland," she confirmed gravely. "'Tis a wonder you didn't cross over to your gods before we got to you, but it seems you're blessed because you still live." She shook her head. "But make no mistake, you need to take great care, as your injury is grave. I applied a special poultice and put herbs in your water to ease your pain, but you *must* remain in bed for now, healing, as your journey back from your deities is not yet complete."

At first, I found her turn of phrase unusual, given our gods were the same, until I saw the cross hanging around her neck. Freya had never mentioned she was Christian, but why would she? It was common enough now for our people to convert, so mayhap it was of no consequence, even for seers, which struck me odd, but it was the least of my worries right now.

"What of Freya?" I asked, concerned about her above all else. "Is she safe? Have you been in contact with her via the flames? Because I could have sworn you told me she was coming when 'tis the last thing she should do."

"I have seen her via the flames, and she's safe." She shook her head. "And no, I said nothing of the sort, for 'twould be unwise given your location. You have been in and out of fevers, so mayhap 'twas your imagination."

Mayhap. But something about the look in her eyes told me otherwise. Yet given my circumstances and her healing me back to good health, I thought it unwise to accuse her of such.

"How did I get here?" I wondered. "The last I recall, I lay on the forest floor looking up at Freya through the trees, then all went dark." Glancing around the room, I frowned. "'Tis clear I'm not welcome, or mayhap I imagined a man's voice as I did your assurance that Freya was on her way."

"*That* you did not imagine," she said. "'Twas Declan Mackay, son of Chieftain Lachlann Mackay, and he can be…difficult."

While I had not heard of Lachlann, the other name sounded familiar.

"Declan Mackay," I murmured, trying to place where I had heard his name before. "'Tis a name that reached our shores, is it not?"

"'Tis," she granted. "He's as well known for his battle prowess in these parts as you are back home."

That's when it hit me, and I raised my eyebrows at her. "Surely *not*." I frowned, hoping I was wrong because if so, my near-death experience was just a holdover to a far worse demise. "Not *the* Declan MacKay, renowned for being King Alexander's most prized warrior? Declan Mackay, 'The Ruthless'? The man who's known to have single-handedly driven our people from these shores? Who has slain countless Norse?"

"*Ja*." She shook her head and looked skyward. "Though I would say the tales are taller than the truth, much like those told of you and mayhap even me and my sisters."

"If 'twas truly his voice I heard on my deathbed, I would say the tales not as tall as you think them," I countered, hardly believing I was in Declan Mackay's castle when his hatred of the

Norse, whether Norwegian or otherwise, was renowned. Yet here Astrid sat acting as though he didn't threaten her in the least.

"And why am I here again?" I asked tentatively, wishing I had more mobility because again, my fate at Declan's hands was not bound to be good *or* honorable. "Better still, how, given my location? You could not have carried me back here alone, nor put me in a chamber that is better than any Scotsman would feel I deserve."

"On that you are quite right," came a man's voice, before the last person I expected to see entered the room.

"I know you," I exclaimed. "You're the merchant on the shore that night." I took in his fine clothing and the blue and green plaid wrapped over his shoulder. "Yet you are no merchant, are you?"

"Nay," the voice I had heard before growled, and another man entered behind him. Tall and formidable, with dark hair and the same plaid wrapped over his broad shoulder, he shot me a fierce scowl and narrowed his piercing green eyes. "He isnae a merchant but Chieftain Lachlann Mackay, and you are here at his bidding because I would have let you die where you were, heathen."

"Which makes me a heathen, too," Astrid reminded softly, yet her gaze was anything but gentle when she narrowed her eyes at him. "And you would do well to remember that, Declan."

"And you would do well to remember—"

"Enough, you two," Lachlann grumbled, shooting his son a disgruntled look before lowering into a chair by the fire. His skin was pale and drawn, speaking to a slow recovery from nearly drowning. He paused for a moment, as if weighing his words, then spoke to me. "'Twas verra risky bringing you here after I heard Oksana had found you, but I owed you a debt for saving my life, Soren Dahl, and Astrid pleaded for your life, so here you are."

"Many thanks," I replied, loathing how vulnerable I was in this bed. Hell, I couldn't even sit up properly and defend myself if these men decided to slaughter me here and now. Or worse yet, drag me to their king, where I would surely be forced to suffer for days to rally their armies' spirits if nothing else.

"What now?" I grunted. What else could I say? My days were undoubtedly numbered, and I would know my fate.

"Now we see you healed," Lachlann said.

Declan stood in front of a window with his arms crossed over his broad chest and glared at me, making clear what he thought my fate should be.

"And then?" I prompted. Pain throbbed in my gut where I'd been stabbed, causing my vision to blur, but I refused to wince and show weakness in front of these two. "What after that, now that you have stolen an admirable death from me?"

"Och, you have some nerve after—"

"Nay," Lachlann cut back, scowling at his son before his attention returned to me. "Now we will wait to hear more talk of what happened at the shore. Right now, 'tis being hailed as the Battle of Largs, as our countrymen heroically drove yours from our land once and for all."

"So our men fled?" I asked. *Prayed.*

"Aye, like the bloody cowards they are," Declan ground out, earning another sharp look from his father.

"Aye, many of your people fled, Soren." Lachlann eyed me curiously. "Lives were lost on both sides, but 'tis said not as many on our side as there might have been given the actions of one berserker Viking warrior as they're calling you."

"Then 'twould be my Viking ancestors working through me, because as you well know, they're of the past now," I said, unsure what he referred to, assuming this was some odd interrogation on behalf of King Alexander. "So explain yourself in terms I might understand, for 'twill soon be known I slayed many of yours to save my own."

"Actually," Lachlann divulged, "I just received more word of the battle, and 'tis claimed you took down dozens single-handedly but didn't kill one." He shook his head slowly, clearly trying to make sense of it. "Your comrades did, but you left a trail of wounded rather than slain. They might not be able to fight for some time, but they now live." A frown settled on his face. "'Tis said King Alexander is offering a reward for this merciful berserker, as 'twas reported by many he was cut down in the battle, yet there is no sign of his body."

"Bloody hell," Declan cursed, shaking his head. "I knew nothing good would come of this." He narrowed his eyes at me again. "If not for you saving my father, I *never* would have allowed it."

"Despite it not ultimately being your choice, son," Lachlann reminded, considering me. "Why didn't you kill those men? 'Tis strange, given the situation."

While I debated whether to tell them the truth, as it might work against my reputation as a fierce warrior, it might be prudent now. Perhaps it would even improve my chances of getting out of this forsaken country alive in the end. Or they could see it as a weakness and find me less of a threat than I already was. Hoping they might show me the same mercy I showed their countrymen, I went with the former.

"Because I never wanted to be here to begin with," I finally confessed. "And I saw no reason to slay men who had done me no harm. 'Tis easy enough to cripple a man in battle rather than take his life. Cripple them enough that your countrymen might stand a chance."

Although I sensed that surprised them, their expressions remained unchanged.

"And your king?" Lachlann prompted softly. "'Tis rumored King Hákon was on our verra shores." His level gaze never left my face. "Is that true?"

What harm could it do to tell them now? "'Tis."

"And now where is he?"

"I couldn't say," I managed, still trying to keep the pain from my face, but it was becoming difficult. Overwhelming.

"Do you suspect he will attack again soon?"

"I don't know."

"Somehow I doubt that," Declan said dryly, trusting me no more than I would him if our situations were reversed. "Given your reputation and that you were among the first boats to come ashore, I would say your king thinks highly of you, so you're closer to him than most. That means you would have a verra good idea what he might do next."

"I agree." Lachlann considered me. "Yet something tells me you willnae be divulging that information."

He was right. I would not.

"Mayhap he willnae divulge it to us," Declan said, his tone mildly threatening, "but I suspect our king could get it out of him." He shrugged. "And we could use that reward, Da."

"Despite him saving your father's life and choosing to wound rather than kill your countrymen," Astrid reminded, frowning at him. "Despite your assurance that you would help see my sister's husband safely back to her."

I could not help but wonder at the look that passed between them. Why would Declan assure Astrid of such a thing? Better still, why would she believe him, given his view of our people? Was there love between them? Or mayhap he returned a favor?

I tried to focus on their conversation, but my pain had grown too intense. Sweat had broken out on my brow despite chills sweeping through me, and my vision had begun to blur.

"I think 'tis best Soren rest," Astrid said before Lachlann and Declan could continue questioning me because I suspected they were by no means finished yet.

"Let us know when he's well enough to speak with us again," Lachlann replied, saying more, but his words sounded garbled now that my pain had grown so unbearable. My pain grew even more intense.

"You must drink this, Soren." Astrid tilted a cup to my lips. "'Twill help you rest and heal."

Doing as asked, I did my best to get the bitter liquid down, yet something told me as Astrid faded and my eyes drifted shut, that my injury would be too grave in the end. It seemed a cruel fate that I might be saved, and possibly see Freya once more, and someday meet my child, yet as I struggled through endless pain, I couldn't shake the feeling that I wouldn't.

After that, I sometimes stirred awake, drenched in sweat and groaning in agony, and at other times, I was at peace, speaking to Freya in my dreams. Holding her in my arms and kissing her lips. She stirred my soul as only she could, promising she would come for me. That we would see each other again.

"I'm almost there, husband," she whispered in my ear. "You just need to wait for me. Stay with me."

"I will always wait for you," I promised, and I would.

Or so I hoped.

Breathing had become more difficult, and Freya's voice more challenging to hear despite how hard I tried.

Was she still talking to me?

Was she still there?

I tried to call out, but I could not. I wanted to tell her how much I loved her, yet it was impossible. A familiar darkness swallowed me, and I knew when I sank into its depths, it was far too late.

CHAPTER SEVENTEEN

Freya

D ESPITE A SMALL storm near the Orkney Isles that slowed us, the winds remained in our favor, and we drew closer to a woodland area I'd seen in my dreams a little over a week after we left home.

"We will lay anchor here and then you will bring me ashore tonight," I told those traveling with us, looking at them in warning. "Despite my sister's presence here, 'tis best to consider this enemy territory, so tread carefully."

It was far too risky trying to hide my boat and those traveling with me ashore while seeking out Soren, so this was our only option. I had wanted them to drop me off alone, but Ivar refused to let me go by myself, reminding me that he was there to protect me and my child.

"How does Soren fare?" Ivar asked me softly, joining me at the front of the boat. "Have you sensed him or heard from your sister?"

Thankfully, Ivar and I had come a long way on this journey, and he was no longer wary or distrustful of me. Rather, we'd spent ample time talking and got along better than we thought we might.

"I sensed Soren, but our moments together in dreams were

fleeting, as if he were only partially with me." I swallowed my emotions because now was not the time for them. Now was the time to stay strong, think clearly, and get to his side as swiftly as I could. Either help nurse him back to health with Astrid or have one last chance to say goodbye. "Little from Astrid other than her urgency that I get there." Inhaling deeply, I tried to keep fear from my voice. "That time is limited."

Ivar said nothing to that, but I didn't miss the concern in his eyes when his gaze swept over the distant shoreline. "If anyone can survive the sort of wound you fear he suffers, 'tis Soren."

"And he will," I vowed. *Prayed*.

Fortunately, although blustery and cold, the waves were not overly big, and the storm brewing in the distance had yet to reach us by the time we made our way to shore. The chilled air smelled of wood smoke from distant fires, and the trill of bagpipes echoed on the wind, but they were far enough away that we need not worry.

After our men dropped us off, followed by Sten when he jumped out after us, Ivar and I kept to the shadows until we were under the cover of trees.

"Now we wait," I whispered when my pendant warmed. Recognizing them from a vision, my gaze drifted to two trees leaning against each other. "Astrid will come from that direction."

Ivar remained silent with his blade at the ready lest someone other than my sister happen upon us. Sten stood at attention, his gaze trained on the woodland and his ears perked forward. Thunder rumbled closer, and the wind picked up as we kept watch and prayed Astrid appeared soon, and that we were not too late.

When my pendant grew warmer still and an overwhelming sense of urgency surged through me, I tried not to panic. Tried not to fear the worst, but it was difficult. All I knew was that I needed to get to Soren soon. Right away. So, when movement ahead caught my attention, I started walking despite Ivar grumbling that I shouldn't.

"'Tis her." I was certain of it. "'Tis Astrid."

Moments later, a slight figure with a dark, hooded cloak appeared through the trees, and our gazes locked on each other. Never so relieved, I rushed to my sister and we embraced, holding on tightly.

"'Tis *so* good to see you, Freya," she whispered. "I've missed you and Tove so very much."

"And I you." Fearing the worst, I met her eyes. "Please tell me Soren still lives."

"He does, but barely," Astrid said, her tone urgent. "You must come straight away." She shook her head and gestured at Ivar and the wolf. "But they cannot. 'Tis far too risky."

"Freya goes nowhere without me," Ivar growled, shaking his head as well. "'Twas the stipulation of allowing her to come to begin with."

"Whilst Freya will be safe enough, I cannot guarantee the same for you," Astrid returned. "Clan Mackay puts themselves in a difficult enough position already with the Scottish king placing a bounty on Soren's head. Whilst they owe a debt to Soren, they won't feel the same about you. And one look at the wolf will mean his certain death."

Ivar frowned. "How does the king know Soren is still here?"

When Astrid looked at me in warning and shook her head that we did not have time for this, I knew Soren was doing poorly indeed.

"There's no time for questions right now." I shot Ivar a look he had gotten to know well on our journey. It meant I knew things he did not. *Felt* things he could not. "If we don't do as Astrid says, I won't be taken to Soren, and I *must* go to him before 'tis too late." I rested my hand on his shoulder. "Please, my friend. We are nearly out of time, and his wife and daughter should be with him. Save him if 'tis a matter of us being there that keeps him with us."

"You cannot ask this of me, Freya," Ivar said through clenched teeth.

"Yet I must," I replied. "You need to stay here and await our return, whether Soren makes it or not. We need to bring him home, and I can't do that if the Scots get their hands on you. Worse yet, if it draws attention to our boat and men."

Ivar considered me for a moment, clearly conflicted and weighing his options. What the best move here was before, thank the gods, he finally said what I needed to hear. "Be safe and bring him back, Freya." He nodded once, solidifying the divide we had finally crossed together. "Bring him home, my friend."

I nodded once in return and looked at Sten. "Take care of each other. We'll see you again soon."

While there was no way to stop Sten if he were determined to follow, it seemed he understood how important it was to remain with Ivar because he remained by his side when I followed Astrid into the woodland. Yet when I glanced back and caught a glimpse of my gray wolf peering at me from the darkness, I suspected Sten followed its bidding, too.

Astrid put a finger to her lips, urging me to remain quiet, and started down a small, hidden path cutting through bushes and ever-thickening woodland, slowing when the sight of a castle emerged in the darkness. After scanning the small distance between us and what appeared to be a back entrance, she gestured that I follow her.

Although we were in the rear of the sizeable structure, what I could see of it looked impressive, with several levels. After entering a dark hallway, Astrid lit a torch she'd pulled from a wall bracket, and we headed up narrow, steep stone stairs, climbing several floors before ascending more spiraling steps into what seemed to be a tower.

At the top, Freya opened a door and led me inside a sizeable room with a warm, inviting fire. Yet all I felt was chilled to the bone when I laid eyes on Soren. With drawn, pale skin, he struggled to breathe, the sound shallow and labored.

My heart in my throat, I dropped my satchel, raced to his side, and took his hand.

"I'm here, husband." Wrapping my fingers with his, I leaned close and whispered in his ear. I could feel the heat of his fever wafting against my skin as if from a fire and smell the sickness in him. "Just as I promised you I would be in our dreams."

Nothing.

No response. No squeeze of his hand.

No stirring of any kind.

If anything, he grew stiller. Then, terrifyingly enough, as if he knew I was here, and he could finally let go, he released a long, rattling breath.

"No," I whimpered, shaking my head, refusing to believe it. Hear it. *Feel* it. "'Tis not time, yet." I kept shaking my head, and did all I could think of when my pendant and talisman warmed against my skin. "I will not allow it any more than you did."

Removing it from my neck, I pressed it into his palm just as he had into mine years ago on my deathbed. Wrapping his hand around it, I rested my cool cheek against his hot, fevered chest and prayed for him to stay with us. Demanded it. Refused to let him go.

"I return the strength of the wolf you gave me so long ago, my love," I whispered, tears leaking from my eyes when I no longer heard his heartbeat.

Yet I kept talking.

Pleading.

Reminding him why it was not the time to drink with Odin in Valhalla.

"And I give you the might of the bear so that it can lead you back to my shores," I said hoarsely. "Back to your daughter so that she might know her father. Be protected by him until she someday grows into a fierce shield-maiden like her mother and grandmothers before her."

I was about to go on when thunder rumbled in the distance, lightning flashed outside, and I swore I heard a thud beneath my ear, so I kept talking and squeezed his hand around the pendant and talisman.

"Come back to us, Soren," I urged, dropping a soft kiss on his dry lips. "Come back to your daughter. She needs you. *We* need you."

As if in response to my desperate plea, I swore I heard another thud.

Then another.

And yet another before Soren inhaled sharply, and his hand tightened around the pendant, as though it anchored him. As if he battled through a storm and refused to let go and slip beneath the water.

Cupping his cheek, I dropped several more soft kisses to his lips, pleading for him to come home to us. Stay on Midgard and grow old with me. I pleaded with such relentless fervor, I didn't realize his eyes had cracked open a fraction until I went to press another kiss to his mouth when I saw him looking back at me. The air rushed out of me from such stark relief, it was a wonder I could find another breath. That I could even speak.

Yet I could and did, never so grateful.

Murmuring a prayer of thanks to the gods, I blinked back tears and managed a wobbly smile, knowing he would be all right now. "Welcome back, husband."

"You came, wife," he whispered hoarsely, worry flaring in his grayish blue gaze. "You are here."

"She did, and she's safe within these walls," Astrid assured from the other side of the bed and then held a clay cup to his mouth. "Now you must drink this, Soren."

Doing as she asked, he gulped it down, and his eyes slid shut once more. Not before he managed a small smile, though, and whispered, "Our daughter is every bit as fierce as her mother."

Even though he must have heard me tell him about her in his fevered state, somehow, I sensed there was more to it. That perhaps he had even met her in some strange way when he hovered on the brink of death between worlds.

After he fell asleep, I noticed color returning to his face and breathed another sigh of relief.

"Praise God, 'tis a miracle," Astrid murmured.

Now that I was free of blinding fear, I realized a cross hung around her neck. I also saw the leather string around her neck, so I knew she still wore her talisman, albeit hidden beneath her dress. While tempted to ask her about the cross or even accuse her of forsaking our gods, when I gazed into her eyes, I did not. Instead, I saw the tides of change upon our lands and felt only thankful to her. She had cared for Soren, undoubtedly putting herself at great risk, and the relief in her gaze spoke to a caring nature that did not deserve judgment.

"Thank you, sister," I said softly, reaching out to grasp and squeeze her hand. "Had you not brought him here and cared for him…" Shaking my head, I brushed away more tears. "I would have never seen him again."

"No need to thank me." She squeezed my hand in return. "As you know, he was well worth saving. Now let's change his poultice, then sit, talk, eat, and catch up."

"I would like nothing more," I replied, shocked when she pulled down his fur blanket, revealing a sizeable bandage wrapped around his midsection. One covering a wound that made my heart stop, because of its size and location. "This should have killed him."

"Ja." Astrid had just begun to remove his bandage but paused. "My talisman is warming." She looked at me. "What about yours?"

"'Tis," I said softly, feeling the warmth of my mystical connection with Soren washing over me. "This is a good sign." I pressed my lips together and fought another wave of emotion. "I'm certain of it."

"As am I," Astrid murmured, nodding. Hope flashed in her eyes after she carefully removed the bandage and washed the wound. "He is very much a fighter. This wound…'tis a miracle in the works." She shook her head. "Mere hours ago, this was red, swollen, and weeping, yet now…" Pressing a hand to his forehead, she breathed a sigh of relief. "Now his fever has broken,

I have a feeling this wound will heal far faster than it should. That he has been truly blessed this day." Smiling at me, she said the sweetest words I had ever heard. "I have no doubt he will live and regain his strength quickly, sister."

I met her smile and helped her tend his wound. After kissing his lips one last time, Astrid and I sat in front of the warm fire, where a light fare of bread, cheese, ale, and water awaited us.

"So they have treated you well here?" I asked as she poured herself ale and me water. "Much was lacking in your last letter, yet I sensed you were safe with this clan, and you've not said otherwise via the flames." I eyed her curiously. "The last I knew, you were here to keep the peace betwixt our countrymen long established here and the Scots, and hopefully find a favorable marital tie to a prominent chieftain."

"And so I am." She sipped her ale and sighed. "Or at least I was before King Hákon invaded these shores. Now 'tis impossible to know what will happen next, as I'm at the mercy of Clan Mackay, who has proven more than hospitable thus far."

When I prompted her to continue, she filled me in on everything I had missed in a vision or in our shared dreams. Soren's fate that stormy night when he'd tried to come ashore at King Hákon's request, then the battle that followed.

"Laird Mackay feels he owes Soren a debt of gratitude for saving him from drowning," she said. "And his son, Declan, feels he owes me the same for keeping him from traveling on another ship that would have traveled with his father's and suffered the same fate."

Thunder cracked, and flames snapped and crackled on the hearth while she hesitated as if reflecting on something. Better yet, on *someone*.

"There is more to it," she went on, "but I believe that's what influences Declan's motives most in keeping Soren's presence here secret." Taking several more sips of ale as if she needed them when speaking of this Scotsman, she paused and shook her head. "Or so it seems. 'Tis hard to know with him sometimes."

"I see," I murmured, having never witnessed my younger sister's cheeks pinken when she spoke of a man, nor seen the fiery glint in her pale blue gaze that I saw there now. "Declan's motives aside, if you're uncertain you have a future here, then should I assume you will leave with me and Soren?" Frowning, I looked at her in warning. "For this country is no place for you anymore, sister."

"Yet 'tis where I need to be," she said softly, gazing into the fire. "Where my fate lies."

Though she fingered her cross, I had a feeling her talisman warmed against her skin at this very moment.

"Are you sure?" I reached over and took her hand, not liking this at all. "Even you, with your diplomatic tongue and hope for an amicable outcome, cannot help things now. 'Twill be very dangerous for you to stay."

"Mayhap," she conceded, about to say more when a light rap came at the door and she whispered, "Yet 'tis where I must be, however rocky the path ahead."

Before I could respond, she opened the door and two men with blue and green plaids wrapped over their shoulders entered. The older man appeared drawn and pale with graying sandy blond hair, and the younger was as large as Soren and just as fierce when his gaze locked on me.

Although the elder of the two introduced himself as Lachlann, chieftain of this clan, it was his son, Declan, who caught my attention during introductions. As broad-shouldered as Soren, he was a force to be reckoned with, and trouble. Although handsome with his auburn-tinted, dark brown hair, chiseled features, and sharp emerald-green eyes, rage filled his heart. While not apparent in his expression, I could see that it churned deep in his soul.

"How does Soren fare?" Lachlann asked Astrid, looking Soren's way with as much wariness and mayhap surprise as Declan. "Although we were convinced he would die this verra eve, he appears to be recovering quite well now."

"He is, and will *not* die," I made clear, going to my husband's side, ready to pull a blade if needed to defend him despite their actions thus far speaking otherwise. "Thanks to you taking him in whilst my sister saw to him." I looked from Declan to Lachlann. "And for that, you have our eternal thanks."

The men eyed me for a moment before Lachlann responded. "'Tis a debt paid and no more." He looked at Astrid. "I dinnae know how your sister managed to get past my warriors, but they will need to be gone from these shores as soon as possible. The search for him has intensified, and I willnae have my king find me harboring the enemy within these walls."

Then he said something that made my blood run cold.

Something that made me hope Soren's recovery was swift indeed.

CHAPTER EIGHTEEN

Soren

"**D**ON'T LEAVE," I cried out when a little girl with fiery red hair, holding a shield, challenged me to follow her somewhere important. Where, though? I felt like I should know, yet it was just out of reach. When she looked over her shoulder as if someone had called her, then raced in that direction, I cried out again, begging her not to leave me. She slowed and glanced back, the look in her gaze daring me to pursue her.

"'Tis all right, my love," came Freya's gentle voice. "I will *never* leave lest you are by my side."

Though I thought for a moment I dreamt once more, when I stirred awake and opened my eyes, it was to her beautiful face. To her loving amber eyes gazing down at me.

"Are you truly here this time?" I whispered.

"*Ja*." She smiled and cupped my cheek. "As are you now."

Tilting my cheek into her warm hand, I knew this was real. My deathbed nightmares were behind me, and the little girl with red hair had brought me back to her.

And it warmed my heart because I finally understood who she was.

I met Freya's smile. "We have a daughter on the way, *ja*?"

"We do." She didn't seem surprised that I knew, despite not

having told me. "She was with me when I called you back to me, and you spoke of her within your fevered state."

While that pleased me greatly, my pleasure was short-lived when I became aware of our surroundings and realized where I was. Worse yet, where Freya and my daughter were.

"'Tis unsafe here," I exclaimed, sitting up despite her and Astrid telling me I should tread carefully. "I didn't want you here." Frowning at Astrid, I shook my head. "You told me I imagined your words in my fevered state. You assured me she wasn't coming, yet you knew she was."

"No, I never said those words to you," she swore. "'Twas undoubtedly magic at work. The connection you share with Freya and your daughter." Astrid shook her head. "I would not have wanted you thinking they were in peril whilst battling such illness." She tilted her head in consideration. "Yet something tells me, despite your worry over them, some part of you held on because you knew they were coming."

"And thank the gods, too." Freya squeezed my hand. "Because it allowed us time to bring you back, husband, just as you brought me back years ago."

"And for that I'm forever grateful," I said softly, squeezing her hand in return, glad to see her safe yet fearful at the same time. "We should leave straight away."

"Soon enough," Astrid assured, seeming to eye me with amazement that I could so comfortably sit up now. "You're safe here until you're well enough to travel. The chieftain has given me his word. He's kept it thus far, too. No harm has come to either of you despite Freya having been here for several days now."

While some parts were hazy, I remembered Lachlann and Declan, and it was hard to believe. Mayhap not of Lachlann, given I had saved his life, but definitely of Declan, and I said as much.

"Even so," Astrid said, "men came by recently asking if they had seen you, and they lied, so 'tis safe to say you need not fear

Lachlann and Declan. I strongly suspect, however, they would prefer you leave as soon as you're able."

I could tell by the troubled look in Freya's eyes that those men searching for me had shaken her.

"I would imagine they do," I replied, no fool. They harbored the enemy and had willingly kept it from their countrymen. And I, being someone who might know King Hákon's plans, no less. Taking in the room and late-day sun streaming through the windows, I frowned between the sisters. "Where are Lachlann and Declan now?" I focused on Freya. "And where are those who brought you all the way to these shores?"

"Ivar, Sten, and our men await offshore," Freya said. "They know you live and are coming home with us. Whilst I remained by your side, tending to you, Astrid has met with Ivar every other night to keep him updated."

I nodded, glad to hear Ivar had traveled here with her. "When does he come ashore again? And does he typically have a set hour?"

"Tonight and *ja*, he does, lest he spies trouble ashore," Astrid replied, urging me to sit forward so she could unwrap the bandage around my waist. "How do you feel, Soren? Because your speedy recovery is remarkable."

"Thirsty and hungry," I admitted, taking stock of my condition. "Otherwise, I feel surprisingly well."

I thanked Freya when she handed me a cup of cold water that I could at last hold on my own.

"'Tis good you have regained your strength so quickly," Astrid marveled, saying the last thing I expected. "Given it's been just under a week since Freya and her pendant, and mayhap your daughter brought you back from the land of the dead."

"Impossible," I exclaimed, shocked by the state of my wound when it was revealed. "I appear to have been healing for many weeks, if not months."

"'Tis a miracle indeed." Astrid washed it. "As of yesterday, I no longer need to apply a poultice."

Freya offered me a soft smile and fingered her pendant. "The gods have truly favored us with this."

"And truly favored us with each other," I said, meeting her smile.

It was hard to believe we had brought each other back from the brink of death, yet here we were, and I could not be more pleased. I would be happier, still, however, when she was safely away from these shores.

"Do you feel ready to stand?" Astrid asked, rewrapping my bandage. "Mayhap enjoy your first meal in some time?"

I had never been so eager to do anything. "*Ja.*"

"Good," Astrid said. "I will give you two some time alone and retrieve water for bathing. Food and drink are already on the table."

"Thank you for all you have done for me, Astrid." I clasped her hand before she could walk away, and met her eyes, never more serious. "Truly. 'Twas very kind of you, my new sister, and 'twill not be forgotten."

"Of course, my new brother," she replied warmly.

After she left, I finally stood, and nothing had ever felt better. Shaking my head, I marveled at it. "I truly never thought this would happen again."

"Nor did Astrid," Freya confessed. "But I knew you would." She lifted her chin in defiance. "I would have it no other way."

"No, I don't imagine you would any more than I would see you lost to me far too soon." I reeled her into my arms and cupped her cheek, cherishing the feel of her against me once more. "We have too many memories yet to make together, wife."

Closing my lips over hers, I kissed her soundly. Deeply. With everything in me, tasting what had been gone from me for too long. Gripping her backside, I pulled her tight against my arousal, wanting more.

"'Tis too soon for that, husband," she murmured, smiling against my lips.

"'Tis not too soon at all." I untied the strings on her trousers. "'Tis past time, and I would feel you again, Freya. Touch you. Hold you."

"Yet you forget where you are," she said softly. "And who might come through our door at any moment."

She was not wrong. It would be unfortunate to find a sword in my back while deep inside her. The Mackays might claim I was free to go, but they could easily change their mind. To that end, I sighed and agreed that it would be best to wait, then sat down to enjoy a round, flat, cake-like bread called bannock and a thick, flavorful vegetable stew. Eventually, Astrid returned with a bucket of warm water and a washcloth, as filling a basin for bathing would draw too much attention.

"We will leave tonight given Ivar will be coming ashore as scheduled," I made clear, washing up after Astrid left again, admiring Freya standing in front of the fire, staring into the flames. "Then we sail back to the Hebrides to see how the king fares."

"You mean to see if the king needs you again," she corrected.

"'Tis my duty, Freya," I said, feeling a twinge of discomfort in my midsection when I pulled on a clean tunic. A reminder that I was still healing. "'Twould be poor of me not to."

"No doubt 'twould." She sighed. "I see nothing alarming in the flames right now, but I feel death on our doorstep again." Shaking her head and furrowing her brow, she seemed troubled. "Yet I cannot see from which direction it comes."

Although unsettled by her words, there was little I could do about them but try to get us safely away from these shores as soon as possible. Fortunately, Freya had brought me a few changes of clothing so I could dress appropriately, and after swinging my black fur cloak around my shoulders, I at long last felt like myself again.

"What I wouldn't do for a blade at my side," I muttered, not surprised that there were none to be found. That would have been foolhardy of the Mackays.

"Soon enough." Freya poured me an ale. "There are plenty on my boat."

I eyed her curiously. "And how did your boat fare on its first long journey?"

"Truly well." She smiled. "'Tis a fine vessel, aided and not hindered, it seemed, by its crack."

She told me how the crack had warmed at her touch, and the winds carried them even faster. How what had seemed to divide us had only brought us back together again.

When Astrid rejoined us, she didn't seem surprised to hear we would be leaving that night. The sun had already set, so it would not be long now.

"I agree with Freya that 'tis unwise for you to stay here, Astrid." I frowned and shook my head. "If for no other reason than 'tis Declan Mackay you will be staying with, and he's not to be trusted."

"Yet here you sit safely in his castle," she pointed out. "Unharmed and free to go when he might have decided otherwise."

"I believe he did," I reminded. "'Twas his father who gave me safe harbor."

"And 'tis his father I will marry to remain safe here," she revealed, shocking us, "whilst trying to keep the peace betwixt the local Scots and the few Norse left that have long called this land home."

"Surely not," Freya exclaimed, frowning. "He's at least twice your age!"

"Women marry men twice their age all the time," Astrid said. "This will be an advantageous marriage, and he's always shown me kindness. Word will be sent to Father, and I imagine he will be most pleased."

"Without doubt so long as you hand over your shield and blade, and vow never to battle," Freya muttered dryly, looking at Astrid dubiously. "And what of Declan?" She narrowed her eyes, as if trying to picture it. "He's to become your son by marriage despite the two of you being so close in age?"

"That, too, happens all the time," she reminded, her voice different now, as if she battled her emotions. "Declan is fine with it. He has no choice."

Although Freya offered no comment, I suspected, by the way she shook her head and continued eyeing her sister with disbelief, that she didn't believe it. Shortly thereafter, when the Mackays joined us and I saw the troubled looks Declan shot Astrid while we discussed her upcoming marriage and the letter we would be giving her father on Lachlann's behalf, I realized Freya might be right.

"We are amongst King Alexander's favored clans, so your sister will be safe under my care," Lachlann assured Freya, nodding once at me, acknowledging me as Astrid's brother by marriage. "You have my word as a Mackay."

Now that we were standing on equal ground, Declan and I continued eyeing each other warily when he wasn't watching Astrid, making clear who the more concerning party was regarding my new sister, and I spoke to it.

"And what of you, Declan?" I narrowed my eyes in question. "Will Astrid be safe under your care when your father is away, as that would leave you in charge, would it not?"

Declan narrowed his eyes in return. "She will be far safer than you soon will be, Norseman, if you dinnae shut your—"

"Enough," Lachlann snapped, his face paler today and his temper shorter by the looks of it. "Part of the reason you're even here is because of Declan's goodwill toward Astrid, Soren, so you need not worry." He glanced at his son. "You would protect her with your life, would you not, son?"

"Aye," Declan confirmed, his troubled gaze lingering on Astrid for a moment before he nodded at his father and scowled at me. "Of course I would."

Although I disliked leaving Astrid behind, the decision was not ultimately mine, so I had no choice but to relent, and soon after, we made our way out of the castle under the cloak of darkness. Lachlann pleaded exhaustion and remained behind, ordering Declan, of all people, to ensure we went directly to the shore and left. Astrid came along too, wanting these last few moments with her sister.

Naturally, Declan kept his blade at the ready as we made our way closer to the shore, muttering something about sizeable wolves and equally sizeable Norsemen.

"So you have met Ivar and Sten?" I assumed.

"Aye." Declan scowled as if the question need not be asked. "Do you think I would let Astrid wander down here alone? There is plenty more danger to be found in these parts than the invading Norse, who have no right being on our shores."

"Yet here I stand," Astrid cut back, her gentle tone only ever seeming to grow heated with Declan. "An invading Norsewoman defended by an ill-tempered Scot."

She was about to say more, but paused when Declan shook his head sharply, having caught the sound of voices growing closer. "Down," he hissed under his breath. Keeping his blade in hand, he gestured that we crouch behind a cluster of bushes.

"Give me a blade, Scotsman," I whispered, loathing being without one.

Declan frowned and shook his head. *"Never."*

Bastard. Though tempted to try to get one off him anyway, there was no time as the voices drew closer. My heart pounded into my throat while we waited. Was this it? Would I be discovered and taken? What would happen to Freya? Our unborn child? I could hardly imagine.

"Right there," Astrid whispered, pointing at two people walking hand in hand along the shore. "'Tis just a couple out for an evening stroll."

"One that verra likely knows the king has placed a reward on the Norseman's head," Declan warned, "so they wouldnae hesitate to report this."

As much as I hated to admit it, he was right, so we waited until they were out of sight before edging closer to the water.

"There it is," Freya said, pointing at her boat heading ashore.

"I see them," I confirmed, relieved that they had not come mere minutes sooner.

Though eager to be among my men again and away from this blasted land for what I hoped would be the final time, I understood Freya might not feel the same, given Astrid's intentions.

"I will miss you, sister," Freya said softly, as they embraced one last time. "Thank you for everything you have done for us." She pulled back, her eyes as teary as her sister's. "I hope you find happiness here and that we meet again sometime soon beyond the flames of our calling."

"And I wish you the same." Astrid rested her hand on Freya's womb, and a soft smile curled her mouth. "I long for the day I meet my beautiful niece, for she will be as strong as her mother."

After I embraced Astrid goodbye and thanked her again, I shot Declan a warning look. "Take care of her, Scotsman, or I will return to these shores and—"

"Remember that he already vowed he would look after her in his father's absence," Freya reminded, slipping her hand into mine. "Now let's go, husband. I long to be on the open sea with you again."

Even though Declan offered no reply other than a scowl, he did give me the benefit of a single nod that he would take care of Astrid, and I believed him.

"'Tis good to see you, old friend." Ivar smiled and clasped me on the shoulder after we moved right along, keeping a keen eye on our surroundings, and boarded shortly afterward. "Very good." He shook his head. "'Tis a wonder you're here, given whose castle you ended up in. Nobody will believe me back home when I tell them Soren Dahl and Declan Mackay were under the same roof and didn't cut each other down."

"'Twas not as if we didn't want to," I assured him while we set to helping the others get the boat past the breakers. Just in the nick of time, too, when we spied lights further down the shore.

"Astrid still stands there," Freya said, watching the coast. "Alongside her Scot."

"Yet he's not hers," I reminded. "Any more than she is his."

"No," Freya murmured, still gazing at the two of them in the distance. "Not yet, anyway."

"So you think the Norns will lead them to each other?"

"I couldn't say other than there's something betwixt them that will make her wedding his father difficult," she replied. "'Twas clear enough in the way they looked at one another when they thought the other wasn't looking." A twinkle of amusement lit her gaze when she looked at me. "Not just that, but he no longer called you a heathen by the time you left but a Norseman, and I don't think that had anything to do with liking you any better."

"'Tis doubtful," I conceded.

Rejoining our men, I let them know of my plans to seek out the king, and all agreed it was a sound decision. They had no more interest in battling on Scottish shores than I did, but we were proud Norwegians all, and it was unwise to be out of the king's favor, so we set sail for the Hebrides only to learn much-welcome news.

CHAPTER NINETEEN
Freya

WHEN WE ARRIVED at the Hebrides, we learned King Hákon had decided to overwinter in the Orkney Isles, so we set sail soon after, in hopes he would not need Soren and his men until next spring. If that were the case, we would head home for the winter if he allowed it.

By the time we arrived a few days later, everyone was ready for a few days ashore, and we soon learned we were a more welcoming sight than we had anticipated. In fact, not only did our men who survived the Battle of Largs greet us on the docks to much fanfare, but King Hákon himself.

"As I live and breathe, is that really you, Soren Dahl?" he boomed, grinning from ear to ear. Although not as large as Soren, he was a sizable man with light brown hair and dark, olive-green eyes.

"'Tis, my liege." Soren introduced me. "Thanks to my lovely wife and good fortune, I survived the battle."

"I would say you did far more than that." He clasped Soren on the shoulder and grinned at him. "You have returned from the grave a hero." His attention turned my way. "Thanks to your lovely wife. 'Tis a pleasure meeting you, Freya Helvig, now Dahl, for I have heard a tale or two about you in my time." He glanced from Soren back to me. "And now here is yet another heroic tale you two can share around the campfire for years to come."

"And what is this tale?" Soren wondered.

"That you and a handful of brave souls held an entire Scottish army at bay," King Hákon praised, "allowing most of us to leave unscathed." He eyed Soren with pride. "And though we didn't make headway this time, 'tis considered a victory given so few lives were lost, and we will return in the spring." He kept smiling at Soren and shaking his head in amazement. "'Tis something else that not one but two Norwegian heroes went up against a Scottish army and lived to tell about it. 'Tis truly a testament to our countrymen."

Soren looked confused as everyone roared in approval at the King's words.

"And who is this other hero, my liege?" Soren wondered, as curious as I.

"Well, Leif, of course," King Hákon exclaimed. His eyebrows swept up, and he kept grinning. "I take it you thought him dead?"

"I did." Soren met his grin. "The last I saw, he went down in battle." He shook his head. "I can't imagine how he could have survived that."

"As 'twas for you, his courage was rewarded with good fortune," the king said. "He was injured, but one of his men managed to get him out of there. The last I saw of him before sending him and his men home for the winter, he was recovering well." He gave Soren a pointed look. "You should send word to him when you can, Soren, as your loss truly saddened him. He carries guilt that he was unable to remain by your side until the end."

"Indeed, I will," Soren said, his voice hoarse with emotion, speaking to how grateful he was that his friend had survived.

"Why don't we go inside, warm ourselves by a fire, and toast to well-fought battles?" the king suggested. "And to friends lost, may they forever dine by Odin's side."

In full agreement, we joined our fellow tribesmen and King

Hákon to enjoy good food and drink. To be expected, we toasted the handful of Norwegians who had fought alongside me and Leif to keep our countrymen safe many times over. Though I knew it frustrated Soren because he hadn't wanted to be on Scottish shores to begin with, he kept it from his face.

When I did not toast with ale but boiled water as ordered by the gods, and the king wondered why, Soren revealed that we had a child on the way.

"'Tis good news, indeed!" The king toasted to us again, noting Soren's sometimes-tentative movements as he took care to mind his healing wound. "'Tis a miracle you survived, Soren. Now you two must tell us your tale for 'tis no small feat surviving a gut wound on Scottish shores."

"'Tis not," I agreed, having discussed with Soren how we wanted to go about this, opting to be somewhat truthful in hopes the king might soften his stance on invading Scotland again. "But the gods were with him and delivered him into my sister's hands. The same gods that urged me to seek him out on the western shores of Scotland."

"Your sister?" he exclaimed. "Pray tell, how is it you have a sister there?"

"My father wished it so that we might forge a marital tie and mayhap find peace betwixt the few Norse left living there and their fellow Scots," I said. "A tie that could help going forward during these ever-changing times."

Soren told him the rest of our tale, omitting a few things. He refrained from sharing which clan had taken him in to protect the Mackays, lest rumors get back to King Alexander, and how Soren had only wounded rather than killed the Scots he'd fought. The rest he shared, in hopes that perhaps King Hákon might realize how merciful some Scotsmen could be. Realize that resuming diplomatic talks might not be such a bad idea.

"'Tis quite the tale," the king granted afterward, saying little more about it as he toasted us one last time and the evening's celebrations resumed.

"We will provide you and your men tents," King Hákon assured us later that evening, before requesting a word with us alone.

When I cast Soren a worried glance as we followed the king into a smaller tent, concerned we might have come across as Scottish sympathizers, he could only squeeze my hand in comfort, hoping that was not the case.

"Please sit." The king gestured that we join him by a small fire. "I have been giving it a lot of thought since you arrived and have come to a decision."

"About what, my liege?" Soren asked.

"About you and Freya, of course," King Hákon replied. "Whilst I assume you found your way here so that you might return to Scottish shores in the spring, I think for now you have done your fair share for Norway." He looked back and forth between us. "So, unless you prefer staying for reasons I cannot fathom, I insist you travel home when you're ready so that you might continue healing, Soren, and welcome your child amongst your tribe."

Careful to keep relief from my face, I, along with Soren thanked King Hákon and after spending a few more minutes chatting, we retired for the evening, glad to see a basin of water had been brought into our tent for bathing.

Yet before we got that far, Soren wrapped me up in his strong arms, and his mouth was on mine. And that's all it took to forget anything but each other for the moment. Wasting no time, desperate for each other, our tongues tangled, and we yanked at each other's clothes in a frenzy, eager to finally feel one another's flesh again.

After I tugged off his tunic, he whipped off mine. The moment I was free of my boots and trousers, I walked him back against our fur-covered cot until he had no choice but to sit. Burning with need, I barely gave him a chance to free himself before straddling him and sinking onto his hot, rigid shaft, both of us groaning in sharp relief and most certainly, intense pleasure.

Mindful of his wound, I ran my hands up his arms and over his broad shoulders, admiring every bit of him. More than that, I cherished the feel of him beneath my fingers, grateful he lived and was deep inside me.

With me.

Loving me as I loved him.

He did the same, caressing and stroking me as if he had been dreaming of doing it since we last lay together. Running his hands up my thighs and over my slightly swollen belly, he fondled my full, overly sensitive breasts, heightening my sensation.

Cupping his cheeks, I closed my mouth over his and kissed him again, grinding and rolling my hips back and forth slowly in a way that built our pleasure swiftly. Gathering me closer so we were skin to skin, he steered my backside with one hand and wrapped his strong hand in my hair with the other, growling in my ear with pleasure, urging me to go faster.

Take more.

All of him.

So I did, and my building need grew so great that when he released a ragged groan and let go, I went sailing over the edge with him, reveling in the sensations coursing through me. The untouchable way he made me feel.

Never so grateful as to be holding each other again, we remained that way for a time, simply breathing one another in. Feeling our hearts beat as one. Losing ourselves in each other until we finally got around to bathing, before returning to bed and making love all over again.

Eventually, we drifted off in each other's arms, stirring awake just before dawn. After making love once more, as desperate as we'd been the night before, we bundled into warm furs and stepped outside into the crisp morning. Our breath hit the air in foggy puffs just as the sun crested the horizon.

"'Twill be a good day for sailing if we wish to leave soon." Soren took in the various shades of purple splashed across the eastern skies. "Though 'twould be better to give our men a few days to relax and enjoy being ashore first."

"Agreed," I said, about to say more when my pendant warmed and the smoky trail of a nearby fire caught my attention. Though people had clearly gathered around it the night before, it was down to embers now. Yet as I felt compelled to drift that way, it sputtered to life, and I knew one of my sisters reached out.

"Is it Astrid?" Soren wondered, understanding my inner seer was at work. Frowning with concern, he remained by my side. "Does she need us to return and get her because we will?"

"No, 'tis not her," I murmured, sure of it. Crouching before the fire, I gazed deeper into flames designed just for me, only to catch glimpses of Tove standing in front of my father's lodge. She appeared to be trying to gather her emotions before her sad eyes met mine within the flames of a nearby torch.

"Father is on his deathbed, Freya," she said, her words whispered across the distance through the crackle of fire. "You should come if you can. He wishes to see you."

However much I thought my love for my father had faded away, given his sour disposition and unreasonable wishes upon my marriage, my chest tightened with pain at the news.

"What is it, Freya?" Soren crouched beside me and gently wiped away a tear I hadn't realized slipped down my cheek. "What did you see?"

"'Twas Tove." The fire fizzled away, and my sister's face vanished in a smoky wisp on the wind. "'Tis the death I still felt coming. My father…and he wishes to see me before he passes."

"Then we will go see him if you wish," Soren vowed. "Straight away. We will leave this very day."

"I do," I confessed, surprised how much I wanted to see Bjǫrn one last time, considering how foul he had become over recent years. How obstinate about my handing over prized weapons to Soren. Shaking my head, I frowned at my husband. "Yet we need not deny our men a few days of rest. They have earned it."

"*Ja,*" he conceded, considering it. "Why don't we ask them what they would like to do and let the decision be theirs?"

That seemed fair, so we rallied them together once they woke, including those who had arrived before us, and asked.

"'Tis all right to say you wish a few more days," I made clear, meeting each of their eyes. "You have done a great deal for me and Soren over the past month, serving your tribe well, so 'tis your right to take this time." I shook my head, meaning every word. "Neither of us will fault you for it."

"Yet *I* would fault us," Ivar made just as clear, looking at me with pride. "You were willing to travel across the open waters of the sea to enemy territory, and risk your life to save Soren, so 'twould be poor of us not to leave as soon as possible so that you might see your father one last time."

"Agreed," another man said, then another, until all were clear that we would leave soon, and there was nothing more to say about it.

Never more thankful, I helped them ready the boats, and we set sail within the hour to calm seas and a wind once more in our favor, this time leading us swiftly back to the shores of our homeland. The other ships would return to our stronghold, and we would continue on to see my father.

"Feel this," I urged Soren when he joined me and Sten at the front of the boat, where the wolf seemed to like to sit, as if keeping watch and warning all away. I placed his hand over the crack. "Yet again, it proves that whilst it once divided us, now it only brings us back together. Not just us to one another, either, but back to our kin and people."

"So it seems," he marveled. The corners of his mouth edged up, and he wrapped his fingers with mine, squeezing with reassurance, seeing the worry in my heart that I kept from my face. "Fear not, wife. We will get there in time."

While my father's stronghold wasn't all that far north of ours, I was grateful he supported me in this when he might have preferred returning to our tribe straight away after being gone so long. I said so, too.

"'Tis true I'm eager to return, yet you forget that our tribes, in their own way, are one and the same," he said. "Your sisters are my sisters. Your father, my father. So we will be there for our father, *you* will be there, so that you might say goodbye."

I could only hope, as we sailed east into a glorious sunrise over a week later, bursting with vivid shades of blues, greens, and violets. All hauntingly familiar colors that stirred me because they were a sign.

"He still lives, Soren." I pointed out the colors of my sister's and my talismans splashed across the sky, as if we three were together now in spirit, because there wasn't much time left. "But not for long."

It turned out I was right. When we approached my father's stronghold, Tove and my father's second-in-command, Knud, already awaited us.

"Welcome home, sister." Tove embraced me on the dock, holding on tight for a moment, her emotions only apparent in the waver of her voice when she murmured in my ear, "'Tis so good to see you again."

"And you." I held on tightly as well before meeting her pale sea green eyes, moist with unshed tears. Moisture she blinked away, undoubtedly determined to remain unaffected and strong for those watching.

"Come," she said to me and Soren. "He has requested to see you both." She looked at our men. "My people will see you settled, as you must be weary after such a long voyage."

Used to the oddities of seers, our men didn't seem surprised by her knowledge, and Soren and I followed her to my father's lodge. Along the way, I spied my gray wolf staring back at me from the misty woodlands as if here to comfort me, and I was grateful. Without doubt, his steady presence infused me with strength.

Though part of me wanted to be alone with my father, another part was grateful for my husband's added strength by my side when we finally entered Bjǫrn's lodge. Upon stepping inside the dimly lit interior, I caught the sickly scent of death approaching and felt a chill in the air that most could not. I was stricken by how gaunt he had grown since I last saw him. How diminished and different than the strong, powerful warrior he once was.

Sitting on the edge of his bed, I kept my thoughts from my face and slipped my hand into his. His fingers were as frail as the rest of him and icy cold, so I wrapped my other hand around them too, trying to lend him some warmth.

My father stirred awake at my touch and his eyes slid open and locked on me. "Freya," he rasped without the disgruntled look that had become so common after his accident. Instead, he gazed at me through the eyes of the father I once knew. The father who adored me and wanted me to be a great shield-maiden, now looked at me with boundless love and pride rather than fear and anger. "You came."

"I did, Father," I said softly, my throat clogged with emotion. "I'm here, as is my husband, Soren."

"*Ja*," he rasped. With pride in his expression, his gaze drifted to Soren where he stood beside me, resting a comforting hand on my shoulder, and then Father looked at me again. "Tove has shared tales of your great feats on Scottish shores." Rare tenderness lit his eyes when he looked at my swelling belly. "And tells of a child on the way." A small smile ghosted his face, surprising me. "Of a shield-maiden daughter who is just as fierce as her mother."

I could not stop the tears from rolling down my cheeks. Where I had feared disappointment in his gaze that it was not a strong son, I saw only pride and contentment.

"She *is* as fierce as I am." Resting his hand on my belly and covering it with my own, I prayed they would give one another strength as they passed each other between worlds. "Just as *I* am as fierce as *you*, Father."

"*Ja*," he murmured, struggling to breathe now, almost as if he had been waiting for me just as Soren had been in Scotland. His gaze rose to my husband. "I release you from your promise, my new son." A tear leaked from the corner of his eye. "I should have never asked you to take her shield and blade…never should have taken that from her…any of my daughters…"

He attempted to say more, but the words died on his lips.

Instead, he breathed his last breath, and his eyes went vacant.

Unsheathing his blade in supplication, Soren dropped to a knee and lowered his head in respect to the passing of a great warrior chieftain. Blinking back tears, I watched Tove and Knud enter and do the same, as Tove undoubtedly felt Father's passing every bit as much as I.

Anguished, I lowered my head over my father and wept tears I didn't think I would shed over his passing, feeling love for him I had thought lost to me. Then I unsheathed my blade, dropped to a knee, and bowed my head as well, honoring him as the great warrior he had been.

After a time, I stood as did the others, and we began a new chapter for our Helvig tribe. The first of its kind, as it turned out.

And nothing had ever felt more right.

━━━━━ ❖ ━━━━━

CHAPTER TWENTY

Soren

WHILE I HAD experienced touching moments in my life, none were as powerful as the passing of Freya's father, the great and mighty Bjǫrn Helvig. Not just his family and me, but the entire tribe, upon hearing the news of his passing, offered their unsheathed blades and fell to a knee. He had been a great man until the end, and it did my heart good that he and Freya found only love and peace together in their final moments.

Then things only grew more powerful when, one by one, after paying homage to Bjǫrn, warrior after warrior raised their heads and looked at Tove as we exited Bjǫrn's lodge, offering their blades to her in supplication.

Usually, there would be more of a process within a tribe to establish new leadership, but it was clear when not just Bjǫrn's warriors, but all his people looked to her with respect that she would be taking her father's place.

"As she should," Freya said soon after, when we went to her lodge so that we might bathe and prepare for a proper burial that evening. "Tove has long been by my father's side in all things. She's the one he looked to and the one who was here most for our people after the bear attack."

"And she best tames Knud," I added, because it was notewor-

186

thy, according to Freya.

"*Ja*," she agreed. "And 'tis no easy task." Combing her hair after we bathed and dressed, her voice grew soft and knowing. "Yet 'tis his task too, as I suspect he tames her as well in his own way."

"So 'tis love betwixt them?" I wondered, taking the comb from her and running it through her thick crimson locks.

"'Tis *something*," she murmured. "Though I cannot say quite what, as both are hard to gauge sometimes, given their role in my father's life."

"A role and fate that is now theirs to fill." I moved her hair aside and peppered soft kisses on the side of her neck. "One that I imagine will only bring them closer together as the Norns did us."

"Without doubt," she said, tilting her head back until our lips met and we lost ourselves for a time in each other.

After the sun set, we joined the village at the shore to send Bjǫrn off to the gods as he had wished, in the way of our Viking ancestors. Brilliant green and blue lights drifted across the night sky, and the seas were calm.

With our wolf, Sten, by our side, I wrapped my arms around Freya from behind, and we watched as they laid him in a small boat, adorned with his favored weapons, and the vessel was set afire by a flaming arrow as it drifted out to sea. Feeling her pain, I held her as silent tears fell, and her father traveled on fiery sparks to greet our All Father.

Afterward, we went to the Helvig's great lodge and spent the evening celebrating Bjǫrn's life with tales of his adventures and battles. It became abundantly clear as the eve wore on that the people looked to both Tove and Knud to lead them, whether they were married or not. I couldn't blame them, either, after watching the two of them together. There need not be love to see they worked well together, and the Helvig tribe needed that most right now.

Eventually, the evening waned, and Tove asked us to join her and Knud alone for one last toast to Bjǫrn, and so that we might talk of Astrid. As expected, Tove didn't seem to feel she alone should speak with us about Astrid, but included Knud as if it were a given.

"Considering you are taking Father's place now, Tove, you should have this," Freya said when we joined them around a small fire in Tove's lodge. She handed her sister the letter Lachlann had wanted delivered to Bjǫrn. "'Tis word of Chieftain Lachlann Mackay and Astrid's upcoming marriage so that we might strengthen ties betwixt our lands going forward."

Tove broke the seal, unraveled the scroll, and read, her finely arched ebony eyebrows furrowing in confusion. "It *does* speak of marriage, but not of Astrid to Lachlann, but to his son, Declan Mackay." She frowned at us. "How do I know that name?"

"'Twas what I said upon first hearing his name," I muttered, yet this made sense, given Freya's assessment of the two before we left Scotland.

"Because Declan is known for his battle prowess," Freya said, a soft, knowing smile on her face. "Yet that battle does not extend to Astrid...not really."

"Though his hatred of the Norse does," Knud said darkly, a storm brewing in his eyes. A response I well understood yet had to counter for Astrid's sake because someday we might very well stand on the battlefield opposite her husband.

"Hatred that still allowed me to heal in his castle," I defended, surprising Freya as I was the last one who would typically champion Declan. Yet it was true, and that had to mean something right now, if there was ever to be peace between our countries. If ever the pointless deaths at the Battle of Largs were to mean anything. Strive toward a purpose. Make a difference.

Then there was Astrid, stuck in the thick of it, her heart in the right place.

"And Astrid is there willingly?" Tove asked Freya, not for the first time. "You are certain?" She shook her head. "Because if she's not, I will sail there myself and—"

"She is," Freya cut her off gently, offering a reassuring nod.

"There's no doubt in my mind that Astrid, as she told you through the flames, is very much where her talisman and the Norns have led her. Very much where destiny has led her so that all goes as it should on Midgard."

"And 'tis no surprise to you that she will be marrying Declan instead of the chieftain, Lachlann?" Tove assumed, looking at both me and Freya. "That this match is not against her will and 'twill only bring her happiness?"

"Neither of us can speak to happiness as that is in the Norns' hands," Freya replied. "As to it being against her will?" That same soft smile hovered on her lips. "Somehow I doubt it, though I do wonder why Lachlann would have lied to us about who she was marrying." She gazed into the flames and thought about it. "Unless he knew something he didn't want his son knowing just yet, such as impending illness, perhaps." She shook her head. "He was not recovering well from nearly drowning."

"I imagine you will know soon enough via Astrid and the flames," I said, agreeing with her theory.

"And what of you, Soren?" Knud grunted, narrowing his eyes at me, still focused on Declan. "What do you think of the warrior Astrid is to marry, given that you have met the man?"

I nearly said he reminded me a lot of Knud himself, but bit my tongue and said what they needed to hear, bluntly, and prayed it was the truth, at least for Astrid's sake.

"However difficult I found him to be, I believe Declan's feelings for Astrid bear a striking resemblance to those you feel for Tove, and vice versa, so *ja*, I think she will be safe in his hands." Although I debated saying more, they needed to know everything. "I also think Freya is right. Lachlann's health is failing after nearly drowning, so Declan may be closer than he knows to becoming chieftain, putting Astrid in a good position, indeed."

When Tove and Knud's expressions grew tense at my implication that they had feelings for one another, Tove handled things with ease, thanking me for my honesty, however skewed it might be regarding her and Knud.

"'Tis good to see you wearing Soren's pendant, Freya," Tove said, changing the subject, yet her voice remained serious if not a touch sad. "I wish I could have given it to you sooner, as it should have always been yours." She noted Freya's stone within. "And that has never been clearer."

She went on to share what had happened as Freya continued recovering from illness after they left our stronghold all those years ago. Though Freya had no recollection of it, given her youth and what she had been through, it seemed her father had taken it from her shortly after they departed. He didn't want it to influence her future marriage, which, at that time, would never have been to a Dahl.

"While knowing that would have once infuriated me," Freya confessed, without any anger in her voice, "it doesn't now." She offered me a soft, knowing smile. "I ended up with the man I was always supposed to be with in the end, so I forgive Father his trespasses. Soren and I had to walk our separate paths to come together as we should and see our Wyrd through. A Wyrd designed by the gods."

I met her smile, never more grateful for the Norns and our Wyrd. "Indeed, we did."

After that, we spoke of lighter things and enjoyed our time together. Yet, as we said goodbye the next day, all knew our country hovered on the precipice of great change that all three Helvig sisters were destined to be part of. So there would undoubtedly be conversations ahead between our tribes about what came next after the winter passed, and we could travel to see one another more often.

This time, when we departed the Helvig stronghold, the sisters embraced, promising they would see one another after the winter thaw. Knud and I shared a mutual nod of camaraderie that I hoped would someday build into a more lasting friendship.

Ivar and our men seemed well rested and eager to go home when we set sail with our wolf, Sten, standing proudly at our side, forever watching over us as Tove and Knud faded into the distance. Though the seas were choppy and the winds frigid and gusty, the way was far smoother than when I last traveled this route with Freya, and our future far more promising.

Unlike the first time, when our boat approached the docks of our Dahl stronghold later that day, Freya had no trepidation in her lovely amber gaze, only excitement as the horns blared, announcing our impending arrival. Things only got better from there when we spied Brynhild awaiting us on the docks, and our entire village roared in welcome from the shore as we sailed in.

"Welcome home," Brynhild exclaimed, somehow managing to embrace both me and Freya at the same time with tears in her eyes after we disembarked. "'Tis *so* very good to have you all back safe."

Smiling and laughing because there was much joy to be had, we embraced her in turn before we, along with our traveling companions, made our way into the village to much happiness.

The journey had not been easy, but we were home and spent an evening rehashing our adventures and telling tales of battles fought and lives lost. Of new beginnings and a future that looked brighter because we were all together again.

"And what of your shield and blade, Freya?" Brynhild asked later that night as she, Ivar, Freya, and I sat around a small fire in the back of my and Freya's lodge near our tree. She looked from me to Freya. "You said your father, upon his death, asked Soren to return them to you."

"He did," I confirmed. "And so, they shall be."

Heading inside, I retrieved the weapons Freya had given me months ago, sank to a knee in front of her, and held them out to her. "As promised, they are yours to wield again as they should have always been, Freya Helvig."

"You mean Freya Dahl," she murmured. Her gaze lingered on them affectionately before she shook her head. "And they are not mine anymore. I carry your mother's shield and blade with pride now. Those now belong to our daughter, may she someday wield them well."

"If 'tis half as well as her mother, there can be no doubt," I said softly, meaning every word as I gazed into her eyes, proud of her in that moment just as I knew I would be every moment for the rest of our lives.

Much still lay ahead, and times changed more rapidly than ever, but we would change with them for the betterment of our country. Our daughter and all our children to follow would be born into a time of old ways meeting new ways, and the time of Scots and Vikings and ancestors of old would eventually fade into the past.

Yet as I carried my wife to bed later that night and made love until we watched the sun rise together, we sensed only good things to come and a bright new future where our great-grandchildren might flourish. A horizon we could never have imagined, given our pasts, but one that would keep Norway strong and peace washing up on our shores far into the future.

The End

About the Author

Sky Purington is the bestselling author of over fifty novels and novellas. A New Englander born and bred who recently moved to Virginia, Purington married her hero, has an amazing son who inspires her daily and two ultra-lovable husky shepherd mixes. Passionate for variety, Sky's vivid imagination spans several romance genres, including historical, time travel, paranormal, and fantasy. Expect steamy stories teeming with protective alpha heroes and strong-minded heroines.

Purington loves to hear from readers and can be contacted at Sky@SkyPurington.com. Interested in keeping up with Sky's latest news and releases? Either visit Sky's website, www.Sky Purington.com, join her quarterly newsletter, or sign up for personalized text message alerts. Simply text 'skypurington' (no quotes, one word, all lowercase) to 74121 or visit Sky's Sign-up Page. Texts will ONLY be sent when there is a new book release. Readers can easily opt out at any time.

Love social networking? Find Sky on Facebook, Instagram, Twitter, and Goodreads.

Want a few more options? "Follow" Sky Purington on Amazon to receive New Release Kindle Updates and "Follow" Sky on BookBub to be notified of amazing upcoming deals.